To Duane,

For filling my life with music

Contents

CHAPTER 1: A BOY AND A DOG
(APRIL 1885)
The darker the night, the brighter the stars.

On the day everything changed, Ty got up when the morning sun filtered through the dirty kitchen window onto the floor where he slept.

He grabbed a chunk of stale bread from the counter, stepped over his pa's dirty boots and empty bottles and headed off to walk along the waterfront before school started.

He counted 322 steps to the tall fir tree; 117 steps to the corner; down the hill, 655 steps; turn, walk 18 steps to the white house.

He liked to count things. He loved to figure out math problems as he walked. Numbers constantly ran around in his head. They were one of the few joys in his life.

He counted on: 17 sand hills on the side of the road; 23 tree stumps; 16 fir trees; 12 steps more and he saw the water.

Ty loved the waterfront. The early morning peacefulness floated in the air. As he walked down the hill, he noticed that the flowers and trees were starting to bloom.

The water of Puget Sound was calm and a greenish-blue. Ty never knew what shade of blue, gray or green the water would be each day. He stood on the rocky beach and picked up a flat stone to skip.

Then he saw the dog.

He sat by a large log that had been washed up on shore, watching Ty with a most intelligent expression. Regarding him, really. Afterward, Ty wondered if maybe the dog wasn't trying to pick out a boy of his own.

"I know you," Ty said softly. The dog cocked his head. "You been wandering around town for the past couple of months, haven't you?" Several stray dogs roamed Tacoma's streets but this one was different. He had only three legs. He was a smallish, tan-colored mutt; young and strong but missing his back left leg. He ran as fast and was as agile as any four-legged dog.

Ty turned back to the water, drew back his arm and skimmed his stone across the surface. Four hops. Seven was his record. The dog watched, apparently liked what he saw and trotted over to him. He sat and looked at Ty expectantly.

"Hungry?" asked Ty. Ty was always hungry, and this dog looked as if he could use some food too. The dog sat, politely waiting. Ty brought out the bread. "Half for you and half for me," he said, breaking it in two. "That's fair."

The dog gently took the bread in his mouth, chewed three times, swallowed, licked his lips, and looked so pleased that Ty laughed out loud.

"OK, I got to get to school," said Ty. "I'll get whupped if I'm late again."

The dog watched Ty walk off and then, a second later, started trotting behind him. Ty grinned.

When Ty reached Pacific Avenue, he heard laughter. Ugly, taunting laughter. Like his brothers'. He looked around and there, down the street, three teenaged boys surrounded a young Chinese man who carried a basket of potatoes.

The boys started chanting:

Hey, Hey!
Chinaman!
Cut your braid
And leave our town!

Then one of the boys shoved the Chinese man so hard he fell off the boardwalk, potatoes rolling out into the dirt street. The boy gave a victory whoop. The young man lay in the dirt, motionless.

Ty froze. Should he run over to help the man? The boys would beat him up too. Why was he

3

such a coward? Ty stood there helplessly, hoping the boys wouldn't look his way. But the boys started pushing each other, laughing, and soon swaggered off. When they were down the street, the young Chinese man slowly got up, sighed, and picked up his potatoes, a resigned expression on his face. He then limped down the street. Ty let out a breath of relief. The dog looked quizzically at Ty.

"Yeah, I ain't so brave," Ty mumbled, ashamed. "Now I gotta get to school." As he started running, the dog trotted along next to him. Ty was puzzled about what he'd just seen. Why hadn't the man yelled at the boys and chased them off, he wondered. That's what Ty's pa would have done. Ty's pa would have beaten 'em black and blue, if he'd caught them.

Ty was so busy wondering that he didn't count one single thing as he hiked up the steep hill to the school. First time ever! He shook his head, thinking he was now counting the times he hadn't counted.

When Ty reached the schoolyard, he turned to the dog. "Can't come in," he said. "Sorry."

The dog looked at him and flopped down under a tree. Would he wait? Ty hoped so. He surely liked that dog.

4

CHAPTER 2: EVA

A crane stands amidst a flock of chickens.

Ty slipped into his seat at the back of the classroom just as the big bell outside of the school was rung.

Thoughts of the dog filled his mind, so it took a few seconds to see that a new girl was in the seat next to him. She was perfectly ordinary-looking, well, except that she had red hair and lots of freckles. But she seemed to crackle energy. She sat at the edge of her chair, her eyes shining. She looked excited to be there. Imagine that! Ty would have been horrified to be the new kid and have everybody looking at him. His whole goal in life was not to attract anyone's attention.

"Class, please welcome Evangeline Doyle," said their teacher, Miss Shaw. "You may call her Eva if you wish. She's just moved here from New York City. That's almost 3,000 miles! Can you believe that, leaving New York to come here!" Miss Shaw shook her head in disbelief, her many chins waggling with each shake.

The girl looked around the class with an eager smile. How many miles away was New York

City? Ty wondered. How long did it take her to get here? He'd liked to figure out that problem. If New York was, say, 2,900 miles away, and she took the train, and the train could travel 37.5 miles an hour....

The problem he was trying to figure out was too big to do in his head, so he took out his slate and piece of chalk and while everyone else was listening to Miss Shaw begin their history lesson, he started writing out long numbers.

He looked up for a second and saw that Eva had turned his way. She glanced down at his slate. Her eyes had a glint of amusement as she looked back up at Ty.

He blushed and put away his slate. Miss Shaw continued droning on about England and some queen.

The school day dragged on forever. When the bell rang, Ty hurried outside. The dog was still there! It barked with joy when it saw Ty and ran to him. Ty marveled again at how easily the dog could run on three legs.

"Your dog is magnificent," a voice said. "How does it balance so well?"

Ty turned to see Eva regarding the dog with admiration.

Ty didn't know what to say. He started scratching the dog's ears.

Eva smiled at him. "Also I couldn't help but notice earlier you were doing some complicated equations."

Ty blushed.

"You're smart, aren't you?

Ty shook his head. He knew the truth. "I ain't," he said in a soft voice. "I can't read."

Eva looked surprised. "You can't read? Why not? Reading is ever so much easier than doing those long problems I saw you do. I learned to read when I was four."

Ty shrugged and looked down at the hole in his right shoe. He was stupid, that was all there was to it.

Eva stood there for a moment, pondering. Then she smiled.

"I have an idea," she said. "Come meet my mother. She can do anything so maybe she can teach you. She's starting her own business. Her friend Mrs. Markham lived in Tacoma before moving to Portland. She wrote us once that no one had a typewriter in Tacoma. So Mother bought a typewriter and we moved here. She aims to make our living by typing up professional letters and documents. She's clever."

7

Ty looked at Eva, dumbfounded. Someone could teach him? The thought was incredible. And she had a typewriter? Ty had only seen pictures of typewriters.

"Can you come right now? Will your mother care?"

Ty shook his head. "My ma died."

"I am truly sorry to hear that," said Eva. "I bet she was a very fine woman."

Ty had no idea if she was a fine woman. She died right after he was born, and his pa never talked about her. Ty had never even seen a picture of her.

"Come with me," said Eva. "Your dog can come too. My mother loves dogs."

"He ain't my dog," said Ty. "Wish he was."

"Well, you should keep him. It's obvious that he's crazy about you."

Ty looked at the dog in amazement. No person or animal had ever been crazy about him.

They headed downtown to Eva's house, with Eva chattering and laughing the whole way. She talked about taking the train from New York to Tacoma and her Manhattan brownstone home and school and how much she loved to read. Ty just nodded. He wasn't a big one for talking, and Eva didn't seem to care in the least. She had lots to say and much to laugh about. Ty tried to think of what her laugh reminded him of. Then he knew: the spring that bubbled up out of the hillside going downtown, clear and fresh and full of life.

As they headed down the hill, Eva noticed the tall piles of sand on the side of the road.

"Why are all these sand hills out here?" she asked.

"Construction," said Ty. "Hills need to be leveled so the houses can be built on flat ground." It felt strange for him to be explaining things to anyone. Embarrassed, Ty ran up one of the sand hills. The dog didn't follow him; instead it stayed down and barked.

Ty looked out to Puget Sound. From his vantage point, he got a clear view of the Olympic Mountains rising like a rugged, majestic, snow-covered castle to the west.

"Look!" he said to Eva, motioning for her to run up too. She shook her head.

"I have eight buttons on each boot," she said. "If I got sand in my shoes, do you know how long it would take for me to unbutton and button my shoes?"

Ty immediately started to figure that out. If one button took five seconds to unbutton and each boot had fifteen buttons, one boot would take 75 seconds to unbutton and then another 75 seconds to re- button, times two boots, which would be...

Suddenly he heard a slight sucking noise and the sand beneath him gave way.

Sand was all around him.

He couldn't breathe.

He'd been swallowed by sand.

CHAPTER 3: THE SAND HILL

*What first appears as a calamity may
later bring good fortune.*

When Eva realized the sand hill had collapsed, she screamed. The three-legged dog barked and dug furiously in the sand. Never had Eva screamed so loudly. "Help! Someone! Help!" She looked around wildly. A Chinese man was walking down the hill, carrying two buckets.

"Help!" she shouted at him. "He's in there! He's going to die!"

The man ran towards the collapsed sand hill. Eva tried to dig with her hands, but sand would immediately fill in every hole she made. The dog had backed away and was whining, pacing.

Then the man was there. He dumped slop out of the buckets, tossed one to Eva and then started to use the other one to dig. Eva's heart pounded as she dug with her bucket. They had only one task, and that was to dig until they got Ty out. Dig it in, fill it up, toss it away. Repeat.

How long can someone live without breathing, surrounded by sand? She dug faster.

Then the dog ran up the hill and started barking.

"It might smell something," said Eva. The man began to dig next to the dog.

"His hair!" screamed Eva. "There! Eva could see Ty's forehead, then his eyes, his nose, his mouth. The man was using his hands now, scraping sand away from Ty's mouth and nose so he could breathe. Was it too late?

Then Eva heard Ty gasp. He gasped for breath, then gasped again. He couldn't get enough air.

The man pulled Ty out, and the boy fell forward, still gasping.

Eva ran over to him. "Ty! Are you all right? Ty! Can you breathe?"

Ty lay on the ground. His eyes were closed, and his eyelids, face, and hair were covered in sand. His chest heaved as he worked to suck in air.

Eva took out a handkerchief and wiped the sand from his face. "You'll be all right," she said. "Just keep breathing." Never had she been so grateful and so relieved.

Ty started to say something but realized his mouth too, had sand in it. He spit a couple of times. And he kept breathing.

Eva turned to the man. "You are a true hero," she said. "You saved Ty's life." This was the first time she was able to really look at their Good Samaritan. He was a short, handsome man who wore the dark tunic and cap that many of the Chinese men in town wore.

The man held out his hands. They were shaking. "A hero who was terrified," he said.

Ty sat up now, coughing and spitting out sand. The man squatted next to him. "My name is Yon Fong Low. Do you need a doctor or anything?"

Ty could only shake his head. He was OK. Besides his pa would never pay for a doctor.

"Mr. Low, do you have a restaurant in town?" asked Eva. "I saw your name on a sign."

Mr. Low stood up. "Yes, for ten years, with my wife. I am overdue there now. One of my waiters just quit, and I must work."

He checked on Ty once more, picked up his buckets and hurried off.

Ty sat there, breathing in and out, his lungs still savoring the sweet, bountiful air. Breathing was the best gift he could ever imagine. He was alive. Oh glory be, he was alive.

"Want me to walk you home?" asked Eva. "I could tell your father what happened."

Ty shook his head. His pa could be drunk or angry or downright mean. Ty didn't want Eva to see that.

The dog who had been sitting and watching Ty now got up and trotted over to him. He sat directly on Ty's feet. Eva laughed.

"He couldn't get any closer to you than that," Eva said. Ty gently patted the dog's head.

"Want me to take the dog home with me?" Eva asked.

Ty shook his head again. The three-legged dog had chosen him. He'd just have to convince his pa to let him stay which, depending on Pa's mood, might be impossible. Well, he had to try.

With the dog next to him, he headed home. Sand seem to shake off of him at every step. When they reached his house, Ty led the dog into the run-down barn, closed the door, and then went to find his pa.

Pa was in the back, chopping wood. That day Ty got lucky. His pa hadn't been drinking, and he was in a good mood. He'd caught a whole mess of fish that afternoon and had eaten his fill. A full stomach does powerful things to a man's temperament.

"Pa, I got me a dog," Ty said. "I'm keeping him in the barn. He's got three legs."

14

His pa didn't even bother looking at him, he just kept chopping. "Ought to kill it. Put it out of its misery," he grunted.

"It don't bother him at all to be minus a leg," Ty said, trying hard not to sound desperate. Pa didn't like it if a person was desperate.

Pa kept chopping. Ty waited. He had no idea what Pa was thinking. Just then Ty's big brothers – Sam and Fred – sauntered up.

"Did you hear?" Pa said to them in between chops. "The fool boy got himself a three-legged dog."

Ty's brothers started laughing. Suddenly Ty had a horrible thought. Sam and Fred might torment the dog like they tormented him.

"Pa, tell them not to hurt the dog," he said. "Please, Pa?"

Pa snorted. Most days he wouldn't even consider adding another critter to the household or to do anything his sons asked, but he felt good that day. What was it to him if Ty wanted to have a dog? He'd had a dog himself when he was a boy back in Minnesota. He kinda liked that mutt. He stopped chopping wood and wiped his face. "Don't mess with the dog," he told his two oldest sons. "Or I'll knock you silly."

Ty stood still, shocked. Did that mean he got to keep the dog?

Sam and Fred guffawed, but they knew their pa would keep his word and knock them around.

"If that dog brings us trouble, I'll shoot it," Pa muttered, picking up the axe and starting to chop again.

The dog could stay! The dog was his! Ty had never felt so happy in his life.

He ran as fast as he could out to the barn. "This barn is your new home," Ty told his dog. "And I'll take care of you forever and ever." The dog looked up at Ty with his big brown eyes and wagged his tail. The boy was sure he understood.

***

In the next few days, Ty spent as much time as he could with his dog. They went to the waterfront, and the dog chased seagulls and splashed into the water trying to retrieve the stones Ty skipped. They walked through the woods, and Ty showed the dog his favorite fir tree which he calculated was over 200 feet tall. They sat together on the hillside and counted the small boats sailing in the waters of Puget Sound.

All the time, Ty was trying to figure out what to name the dog. It was important to find just the right name. Ty had never had such a big decision before. He pondered possible names for a long time.

The dog had three legs, not four, so he was minus one. Minus sounded like Linus, and Ty once knew a farmer named Linus Seeger. "Minus," said Ty. "That's it. I'm going to name you Minus." At that the dog looked up, sneezed, and thumped his tail twice.

"See, you already know your name," Ty said proudly and went over to scratch his head.

Minus leaned into Ty, relishing the scratches; then he sank to the ground in bliss, closing his eyes and turning over on his back so Ty could scratch his stomach. Ty laughed out loud at his dog's expression of pure joy. "Me too," whispered Ty. He had never been so happy.

CHAPTER 4: MEETING MRS. LOW
Hoping for a pearl from an old oyster.

A week after Ty adopted his dog (or the dog adopted Ty), Ty met Eva's mother. Eva had not forgotten what their mission had been on the day Ty was swallowed by the sand hill. Every day at school, she'd pester Ty to come home to ask her mother for help. Finally he agreed, and after school one day they headed past that fateful sand hill to Eva's house.

"Do you think you can teach him to read?" Eva asked her mother. She was a tall, slim woman with auburn hair streaked with gray.

Mrs. Doyle looked at the ragged, dirty boy and then at her daughter's eager face. "Does she think I'm a magician?" she thought with dismay. "Little does she realize how unmagical I am."

"Well?" asked Eva.

"I honestly don't know," Mrs. Doyle said. Her daughter's face fell. Mrs. Doyle quickly said, "But of course we can try. When school lets out for the summer, we'll set up a schedule. I bet we can do it." As soon as she said that, she regretted it. She didn't want to disappoint her daughter or the hopeful boy. Trying is one thing, succeeding is another. And she had her hands full just trying to start a typing business.

Eva looked at Ty triumphantly. "See, I told you," she said. "Once summer comes, you'll be reading in no time."

***

"You'll be reading in no time."

For the rest of the day, those words kept going around and around in Ty's head. Maybe by the fall, when school started again, he'd be able to read. Was that possible? It was his greatest desire. If he could just read, he wouldn't be so stupid in school. The other kids wouldn't laugh at him or ignore him. He wouldn't feel so ashamed.

Another thought kept going around in his head that afternoon too. He needed to thank Mr. Low properly for saving his life. In thinking back over the day he almost died, he realized he hadn't thanked Mr. Low at all. If it wasn't for Mr. Low, Ty wouldn't be alive. He wouldn't have a dog of his own. He wouldn't have Eva as a friend. He wouldn't have the opportunity to learn to read. Why hadn't he thought to thank him? How would he go about doing that? Ty always wanted to slip by unnoticed, so talking to

Mr. Low was going to take some effort. But when someone saves a person's life, well, that person needs to acknowledge it, doesn't he? Ty made up his mind. He would go to Mr. Low's restaurant. He'd thank him and give him the one treasure that he valued over everything else, except Minus, of course, and that was a completely whole, wonderfully beautiful sand dollar that he'd found on the waterfront.

Ty kept the sand dollar on a shelf in the barn. On the Saturday one week after he was rescued, he carefully took the sand dollar and one last time marveled how nature had perfectly etched a design that looked like a wild fern onto its top. Then, with Minus trotting by his side, he hiked down the hill to the restaurant. He was still amazed at how easily Minus ran on three legs. Clearly, he was a clever and extraordinary dog.

Down on Pacific Avenue Ty found Mr. Low's restaurant. Eva had told him exactly where it was. "You stay out here," Ty told Minus. "I'll be back soon." Minus sat and looked at him expectantly.

For one second Ty stood outside the restaurant, trying to get the courage to go in. Then he remembered Mr. Low pulling him out of the sand hill and how grateful he was to be alive. He took a deep breath and nervously pushed open the door, stepping into a different world. He'd never been in a restaurant before. He stood in a large open room with round tables covered with white linen tablecloths. Colorful paintings of delicate flowers and birds decorated the walls.

It was mid-afternoon so the restaurant was empty. Ty could hear people working in the kitchen, but he couldn't see anyone. He took two more steps into the restaurant and smelled the wonderful aroma of food cooking.

Just then Mr. Low came out of a room in the back of the restaurant. He recognized Ty immediately. "Hello!" Mr. Low said. "You are the boy from the sand."

Ty blushed and held out his shell. "This is for you," he said, trying to remember the speech had had prepared. "I wish to thank you very much for saving my life."

He handed the sand dollar to Mr. Low and looked at him expectantly.

"Ahhh." Mr. Low recognized that this was a special gift indeed. "Thank you."

Mr. Low looked at the scrawny boy and asked, "Would you like to have a cup of tea and some refreshments?"

Refreshments? Food? Ty never turned down food. He nodded shyly.

"Please come. My wife and I always have tea at this time," said Mr. Low, motioning Ty to follow him. He led him to the office in the back of the restaurant. There propped up on the sofa, covered with a light green silk comforter, was a woman who looked like a bright sparrow. She was surrounded by stacks of books, papers, a chess set and other intriguing odds and ends. Her sharp, sparkling eyes took in Ty.

Mr. Low said something in Chinese. She answered him and laughed.

Mrs. Low lifted a hand in greeting, much like an elegant queen. Her eyes had a touch of mischief. "Mr. Low said he uncovered a buried treasure," she said. "And it was you!"

Ty blushed and once again didn't know what to say.

"He gave me this," Mr. Low said, holding up the sand dollar.

Mrs. Low examined it closely. "Never have I seen such a shell," she exclaimed. She looked up at her husband. "Mr. Low, I don't think you can accept such a valuable gift."

Ty's eyes got wide. "But he has to! I want him to have it!"

"Then we can't possibly turn it down," she told her husband. "We shall give it a place of honor on my desk."

"I agree, Mrs. Low," said her husband. And then he placed it in the center of the desk. "Now please, sit," he continued, motioning Ty to a chair near the sofa. "I shall get the tea."

Ty sat on the chair and wondered what, if anything, should he say to Mrs. Low. She was regarding him, sizing him up, her eyes seemed amused. Why was she lying on the couch? Maybe she couldn't walk. Did her legs not work? Was she weak?

Finally he asked softly, "Are you sick?"

Mrs. Low shook her head. "Oh no," she said. "I'm gambling."

Ty was confused. Gambling? How could she be gambling? There was no one else around to gamble with. He didn't see any money or cards or dice.

Mr. Low came in then carrying a tray with a tea pot, cups, a plate of rice crackers, and a wet washcloth.

"Am I not gambling, Mr. Low?" Mrs. Low asked her husband. "Lying here?"

"You are teasing him," Mr. Low said. He turned to Ty. "Mrs. Low is expecting a child."

23

This answer was even more confusing. Ty had seen many women who were expecting babies. He had seen people gambling too. This didn't look like either of the things.

Mrs. Low saw his confusion. "We have long wanted children," she said. "When we came to America fifteen years ago, we had many disappointments. Now Fate dangles our heart's desire before us once again. The doctor suggested that perhaps if I stay reclined, we will get the answer to our prayers. He said it may help, it may not. Nothing has worked before. Why not try the doctor's idea?"

"My gamble is that by lying here, bored to death, this baby will grow and thrive," Mrs. Low continued. "Six more months of reclining is my gamble. As the proverb says, 'A patient woman can roast an ox with a lantern.' I'm amazed at how long a day is, even after I'd done all of the restaurant's accounting and business planning. So much time is left over to think. And read! I've already read so much. I am now memorizing Chinese proverbs and poetry. If you can think of other stationary pastimes I'll gladly do those too."

Mr. Low handed Ty the wet washcloth. "For your hands," he said. "Rice crackers taste better without dirt." While Ty scrubbed his hands, Mr. Low poured Ty a cup of tea. Then he offered him a rice cracker. Ty stuffed three of the crackers into his mouth.

Mrs. Low noticed. "Ah, an appetite! Eat more," she said. "We have plenty."

Ty ate two more and then shyly asked, "Can I take one for my dog? He's hungry too."

Mrs. Low looked at the earnest boy. "I have a better idea. Mr. Low, take him to the kitchen. Cook will have beef bones and table scraps. All dogs love a good bone."

"Mrs. Low, you amaze me with your insight," said Mr. Low.

She waved her hand. "Thank you, Mr. Low. Every day I lie here and gain more insights and wisdom. Today I learned: 'A curious woman is capable of turning around the rainbow just to see what is on the other side.'" Then she turned back to Ty. "Next time you come back, please bring your dog. Heaven knows I long for distractions. Today I have balanced the books three times. I am now changing numbers just so I can find mistakes."

Mr. Low led Ty to the kitchen. Ty almost gasped at the wide array of food being prepared by the cook. He never had enough to eat, and seeing all of this food was staggering. Chickens were stewing, rice was cooking, soups were bubbling away. A young Chinese man was chopping up carrots and onions. A cook was making dumplings. The rich, hearty smells made Ty's mouth water.

Mr. Low spoke to the cook in Chinese, and the cook nodded seriously, wiped his hands on a towel, walked away, and came back with bones and food scraps wrapped up in paper.

Ty could hardly believe his luck. Feeding Minus was a problem that he hadn't been able to solve. Since he himself was hungry most of the time, he didn't have much extra food to give his dog. He knew that his pa wouldn't let a dog around his property if he thought it'd be eating his food. Ty wondered if it ever crossed his pa's mind that a dog needed food. Or that a boy needed food, for that matter.

"Come by tomorrow if you want more. We usually give it away for slop," Mr. Low said. "Come by anytime."

Ty was overwhelmed. No one had ever given him anything. Ever. "I can sweep or wash dishes or anything, if you need help," he said.

Mr. Low regarded the boy. How much could this raggedy boy help? A restaurant is a busy place. Mr. Low was a busy man. He didn't really have time to babysit a child. Still, his wife had taken a liking to the boy. Perhaps he could amuse her. He said to Ty, "We'll try it and see. Thank you."

So Ty came back the next day.

"First thing you must do when you get here is to wash your hands," said Mr. Low. He wanted to tell the boy to take a bath, but clean hands were a start. "Restaurants must be very clean."

Ty was sweeping the hallway when he heard Mrs. Low's voice coming from the office. She was yelling angrily.

Was Mrs. Low all right? Did she need help? Should he go in? Ty cautiously poked his head through the slightly opened door.

Mrs. Low was alone in the room, lying on her couch with a chessboard on a little table in front of her, looking irritated. Her expression changed when she saw Ty. "You heard me yelling?" she asked. "I am playing chess against myself. I pretend to be two different people. Sometimes they are bad sports. The good news is one of me always wins."

Ty couldn't tell if she was making a joke or not. Then she held up a wooden frame with beads on wires which was lying next to her on the couch. "Have you ever seen this?" she asked, moving a few of the beads.

"What is it?" asked Ty, stepping into the room for a closer look.

"An abacus. A Chinese way of counting."

Counting? Ty immediately was interested. He looked at the contraption. How could it be used for counting?

Mrs. Low beckoned him to come over. "I show you now," she said. Her fingers moved the beads quickly. "You can add, subtract, multiply, divide," she said. She demonstrated each procedure.

"I use it to keep track of our money," she said. "How much the restaurant takes in, how much expenses are." Again, her fingers quickly flicked the beads. She was fast at this little device.

Ty looked up at her, impressed. He'd love to get his hands on that thing.

"I see in your eyes that you are interested. Perhaps we are alike," she said. "Perhaps we both have mathematical minds." And she handed over the abacus to Ty so he could figure it out.

***

Stopping by Mr. Low's restaurant to get table scraps for Minus and chatting with Mrs. Low soon became Ty's daily after-school ritual. He continued to do chores around the restaurant, usually sweeping in the back rooms or taking out the garbage. Ty was proud that he could help.

He quickly saw that he could eat the restaurant's leftover food as well as Minus. To a near-starving boy, the restaurant's scraps and leftovers were a much-appreciated feast. Some of the flavors were new to him too and extremely delicious. The food was an introduction to Chinese cuisine: rice, noodles, and various stir-fried meats and vegetables.

After Ty would pick up the scraps, he and Minus would walk to the waterfront, sit on a log, and unwrap their meal. Sometimes Ty wondered how Minus had survived before meeting Mr. Low. For that matter, how had he?

Visiting Mrs. Low was the first thing Ty usually did when he got to the restaurant. She had Mr. Low bring them tea and rice crackers, Ty would wash his hands, and while he ate, she began talking.

Ty didn't always understand her but she didn't seem to mind. She spoke English very well, but still, she had an accent and if she didn't know the English word, she'd either make it up or use a Chinese word. She insisted Minus come to the office too, and she'd slip him little treats. Minus would eagerly wolf down these goodies and then patiently endured the rest of the hour, sleeping right by Ty's feet.

One day Mrs. Low said, "Enough of my chattering. Today I'm going to teach you chess. It is a game you will enjoy, a game where you can use your mind, a game of strategy, logic, and insight. I need an opponent."

She had the chess set on the table next to her. "Hold them. Feel them," she said. "They're hand carved."

One by one, Ty examined the chess pieces. They felt heavy and elegant to his rough fingers. He especially liked the pieces that looked like horses.

"In China my father taught me a variation of the game," Mrs. Low said. "When we came here, I learned this version."

She took the pieces from Ty and held up them up one by one. "The little ones are pawns. The horses are knights. The bishops have a slash or a cross on the top and the rooks look like little castles. The king is the biggest, but despite his size, the queen is the most important and powerful. Much like in real life where the woman is stronger." She laughed.

It didn't take Ty long to learn the rules of the game. Mrs. Low had been right, chess was a game that was meant for him.

Mr. Low poked his head into the room as they were playing their first game. "Two fine minds engaged in battle," he said. "Ty, I am grateful that you help Mrs. Low pass the time. Otherwise she would be worrying or thinking of new ways to improve our business and new dishes for our poor cook to make. Thank you."

Ty was surprised. He'd never done anything before that people thanked him for.

Just then they heard glass breaking. It came from the front of the restaurant. The cook shouted something. Mrs. Low clapped her hands angrily and said something fierce in Chinese.

Mr. Low replied in Chinese and then left the office.

"The window! Someone broke the front window. This is the third time!" Mrs. Low told Ty, furious. "Once someone threw a big rock, the second time with a brick. What was it this time?"

"Why are they breaking your windows?" Ty asked.

"They want us to leave," she said. "They want our restaurant to close and for us to leave town."

"Who?" Ty asked.

"Someone who doesn't think we Chinese should be here," Mrs. Low said. Then she said something angry in Chinese and threw her pillow on the ground for emphasis.

She took a deep breath to calm herself. "There's a group led by Jacob Weisbach, the mayor here, that says we are taking jobs away from white people. Tell me, how many white people want to start a Chinese restaurant?"

"What can you do?" asked Ty, suddenly afraid that his new friends would leave him.

"Replace the window," she said with a sigh. "And then curse the devils who are doing this." With that, she said another long string of Chinese words. Ty was pretty sure they were swear words.

They could hear Mr. Low sweeping up the glass from the other room. Mrs. Low shook her head. "If I could, I would go after those people. My body must stay here on this sofa now but my brain flies all over, like the black crow outside my window. This couch is my jail. I hate it. When this baby is born, I will hand the child to Mr.

Low, take an axe, and chop this couch into a million pieces. It is an old Chinese custom – to reduce to rubble that which offends you." She laughed and shook her head again.

"Even though we are attacked, I still laugh," she said. "My father said that laughter is the music of your soul. He was a man of surprises. Most fathers in China heap attention on their sons. I have three brothers, yet I was my father's favorite. He taught me chess and how to read and write. But the best gift he gave me?" She paused dramatically. "My feet."

Ty glanced quickly at her feet but they seemed perfectly ordinary. Her slippers were off, and she wiggled her toes.

"Yes, he gave me my feet," she repeated. "He refused to let my feet be bound. Most girls from wealthy families like mine have bound feet. Have you heard of bound feet before?"

Ty shook his head.

"In my country, when girls are very little, their toes are bent under their foot. The bones are broken and the feet don't grow. As grown women, they have tiny, painful, crippled feet and can only hobble."

"Why?" Ty asked, alarmed.

"Tiny feet are a sign that women are rich enough not to work and must be taken care of. Men find it attractive. Dainty. But my father said, 'How silly to ruin my daughter's feet! Let them grow as big as boats.' My mother had bound feet, and she wanted me to have bound feet too. She wanted me to be acceptable for fear I would never marry. Lucky for me, Mr. Low agreed to marry both me and my big feet. Lucky for Mr. Low that my father taught me how to think. How would my husband manage now without me? As the proverb says, 'Man is the head of the family, but woman is the neck that turns the head.'" She laughed again and then made a face.

"The other Chinese women in this town all have bound feet," she said with disdain. "They don't venture out, they don't make decisions, they don't think for themselves."

Then she became serious. "Ty, you must always think for yourself too."

Ty nodded but was confused. Who else could he think for?

***

As Ty was getting to know Mrs. Low and Mrs. Doyle, for the first time in his life, he started wondering about his own ma. He knew nothing about her.

One night, as Ty took his blanket to sleep in his usual spot by the kitchen stove, his brother Fred came in. When Fred was young, before he turned 13 and dropped out of school, he and Ty would play games and explore the woods together. As Fred got older, though, he became increasingly like Pa and his brother Sam.

Sam and Fred looked more like Pa every day; they were big, burly and blonde, with fair skin that burned easily. Ty figured he looked like his ma because he was small and dark, with brown hair and brown eyes. His ma had died when he was just one month old. His brothers, to tease him, would often say she took one look at how ugly Ty was and died right then. Ty certainly hoped that wasn't true.

Tonight Ty hoped his brother would answer a question. "Fred, do you remember anything about our ma?"

Fred stood by the kitchen table and turned to look at Ty. His expression changed, softened, and he looked away. "I remember her singing. She'd sing to me and Sam at bedtime, and she'd sing when she cooked. She sang so pretty." He paused for a moment, remembering, and, as if it was too much, he shook his head and bounded up the stairs to the attic.

His pa came into the kitchen then. He hadn't gone down to the tavern yet, so Ty thought he'd take a chance and ask him a question too. "Pa, what was my ma like?"

Pa frowned. "She thought she was better than me," he said in a low voice. "She wasn't. She always wanted me to change. To give her purty things. And talk nice to her. Well, that ain't me." His jaw tightened in anger. "She coulda treated me better too."

He turned and left, leaving Ty to puzzle over exactly what he meant.

CHAPTER 5: FINDING LI

In the land of hope, there is no winter.

Ty, his pa, and brothers lived in a drafty, hastily built house, originally rented to the lumberjacks who worked in the nearby woods. When the lumberjacks left for other jobs, the owner rented it to a succession of farm workers and laborers, the latest of whom was Ty's pa. The barn on the property was nothing more than a large shack, but it sheltered – more or less – any livestock the renters managed to keep alive.

In the summer when it was warm enough, Ty slept out there. Even though the hay was old, morning sunlight would stream through the cracks in the ceiling and make the place almost magical. At night, as he lay on his back and looked up, he could sometimes see white stars like pin pricks on tar paper far up above in the black sky. Of course, he counted them.

It was the beginning of May now, almost warm enough to sleep out there, but not quite. Every night Ty would put Minus into the barn and every morning, he'd let him out. When he threw open the barn door before school, Minus would be right there, his tail wagging, his body squirming, as if a miracle had just walked into his life. Ty loved that dog more than he ever knew possible.

One Saturday morning, Ty opened the door and said, "Minus, you and me are going down to the waterfront to explore." Minus joyfully turned in circles. Ty knew his dog could understand everything he said. Such a smart dog, smarter than most people, Ty thought.

On this clear morning, Mount Rainier gleamed large and white. Off in the distance were the Cascade mountain range on one side and the Olympic mountain range on the other. Ty walked down the hill, looking down at the water of Puget Sound. Today it was blue-green.

Ty reached the waterfront and watched the water lap the shore. Gulls cried as they swooped down from the sky.

Minus ran around the rocky beach in exuberant joy, his tongue flopping outside his mouth, almost looking as if he was grinning. Ty stopped to look for round skipping stones. Maybe today would be the day he'd skip it eight times.

Over by a pile of driftwood, Minus started barking fiercely. What was that dog up to? Had he cornered some kind of critter? Ty ran to find out.

"What is it?" Ty asked. Then he heard an odd noise, like a moan. He looked behind the log and – there was a girl, a Chinese girl, sprawled in the sand. She was groaning, tossing and turning. She didn't seem to see him.

"Hey!" Ty called softly.

She moaned again and thrashed.

"Are you all right?" Ty whispered. The girl's eyes opened but they didn't focus. What should he do? He counted her breaths. They were fast and shallow.

Ty had to do something, right away. The tide was due to come in soon. He couldn't leave her there for long. But what should he do? Eva! Eva would know. "I'll get help," he told the girl. She moaned.

"Minus, stay here and guard her. Stay."

Minus sat, his tail wagging. Ty, hoping Minus could be trusted as a guard dog, took off running.

***

Eva was surprised when she opened the door early that Saturday morning to see Ty on the other side.

"Good morning," she said. "You're up early."

Ty tugged at her sleeve urgently. "She's sick. A girl. On the beach. Hurry."

Eva woke up fast. "A girl? Mother should come. She helped my father many times in his medical work."

Mrs. Doyle was already in her parlor office, typing, but when Eva burst into the room and told her about the girl, she said, "Let's hurry." She grabbed a sweater, and they quickly left.

Minus was still watching the girl when they arrived at the beach. She hadn't moved at all. Her eyes were closed, her face contorted in pain.

"Merciful heavens," Mrs. Doyle whispered. She ran to the girl and felt her forehead. "Why, she's burning up," she said. "We have to get her out of here and into a proper bed."

Mrs. Doyle took off her sweater, folded it around the girl, and lifted her up. "There's nothing to her," Mrs. Doyle said softly. "She's so light."

It was an odd parade that hurried back to Eva's house. Mrs. Doyle carried the girl. Eva ran after them, and Ty and the three-legged dog followed.

As soon as they reached the house, Mrs. Doyle took the sick girl into the spare bedroom and laid her on the bed. She sent Eva to get a pan of cool water and a towel. When Eva returned, Mrs. Doyle proceeded to sponge off the girl's face.

Eva and Ty stood by the door, watching. Then Eva turned to him with wide eyes and whispered, "Ty Ritter, you just attract excitement. First you find a three-legged stray. Then you almost die in a sand hill. Now you rescue a sick girl." Ty was baffled. He had never attracted anything or anybody before. What was happening?

Carefully Mrs. Doyle sponged the girl's face and hands, arms and legs. Her left arm, twisted at an unnatural angle, had a deep, ugly cut by the elbow. "That arm is broken," Mrs. Doyle said. "I must fetch the doctor. You two will have to take care of her."

Eva quickly moved next to the girl and continued wiping her face. Mrs. Doyle left, and Ty sat down at the foot of the bed with Minus at his feet. The poor girl in the bed looked so fragile. At first, because she was so small, Ty thought she was around their age, but up close, he saw that she was older. Eighteen or twenty? Her long black hair was matted with dirt and blood. She wore a dark blue silk blouse with embroidered flowers and dark blue silk trousers, but they were ripped, stained, and dirty. Despite the sponge bath, the girl was still filthy. Scratches, cuts and bruises covered her face and arms. Her bare feet were calloused and dirt-encrusted.

It seemed forever before Mrs. Doyle returned with Dr. Schneider. When the doctor saw the girl's arm, he swore under his breath. He gently examined the girl, shaking his head and making little noises of displeasure.

"Badly broken arm," he muttered, glaring at Mrs. Doyle as if it was her fault. "Infected. Possibly blood poisoning. Malnourished too. A mess. Not much we can do. Just wait. No medicine I know of can help her."

His face softened as he cleaned the girl's wound and set her arm in a cast.

"Bad break of the arm," he said, almost to himself. "Bad, bad, bad. May not heal straight. May not be able to use it. Well, we'll deal with that later, first she's got to live. The poor girl's got to live."

He clicked his bag shut and stood up. "I'll check on her tomorrow," he muttered. Mrs. Doyle gave him a few of her hard-earned dollars and then he left, mumbling to himself and shaking his head sadly.

Mrs. Doyle sat next to the girl and stroked her forehead. "You're safe with us," she whispered. "We'll take care of you." Then Mrs. Doyle turned to Eva and Ty.

"It's possible she only speaks Chinese," Mrs. Doyle said. "I'll get Mr. Low to come talk to her. Poor girl. She probably has no idea where she is or what's happening." She tucked the quilt up under the girl's chin and quickly left.

Ty sat back down in the chair and watched the girl. It seemed like she was barely breathing. Then she'd give a moan. Ty wondered who she was. Why was she here? Was she running away from something?

Eva, too, seemed to be wondering the same things. "Perhaps she is a princess who has been exiled because of her love of a peasant farm boy," she said softly. "She may have been sent to a desert island and tried to escape by boat but was blown off course and landed here."

Ty looked at the poor girl in wonder. Could that story be true?

Eva thought a bit more. "Maybe she is a performer in a famous Chinese dance troupe that is touring the world. Perhaps the troupe's ship was attacked by pirates, and only she escaped, floating on a log, that very log that we found her by, washed ashore here."

Ty turned to look at Eva now, amazed by her imagination. Her mind was so different than his. Ty looked back at the girl and began to count her breaths. How many breaths does a person take in a lifetime? How many times does a person's heart beat? How many miles had the girl traveled, and how far from home was she?

Mrs. Doyle returned with Mr. Low. He carried a small bottle.

Mr. Low immediately went to the girl's side and spoke to her in Chinese. Her eyes fluttered but they did not open. Mr. Low turned to them and held up the bottle.

"I met Ing Hay, a Chinese doctor, in Walla Walla two years ago," he told them. "He is famous among the Chinese in the Northwest. He has medicines concocted from herbs that cure many illnesses. Patients call the medicines Doc Hay's sacks of bitter weeds. It may help."

Mrs. Doyle spooned some of the liquid into the girl's mouth. Then there was nothing to do but wait, repeat the dosage that night and the next day and wait some more.

CHAPTER 6: LI'S STORY

**Perseverance is the water
that wears away the stone.**

When the girl woke up, she was confused. Where was she? How did she get there? She struggled to lift her head to look around. A bedroom? Was that a small boy sitting in the chair across from her? Was there a dog lying at his feet, snoring?

The effort of trying to sit up exhausted the girl, and she fell back, with a groan. She heard the boy come over to the bed.

"Hey," she heard his soft voice say. She opened her eyes again.

"Where...?" she asked with effort.

"She speaks English," another voice said. The girl squinted and could make out someone with red hair. Then the dog came over to the bed. The girl closed her eyes.

"That's OK. Sleep," the boy said. "We'll be here."

As the girl drifted back to sleep, she remembered the little cabin boy on the ship. Was he the boy sitting there? Did he want help cleaning the

pots and pans? Did the captain punish him
again? And then she fell asleep.

***

Day by day, the girl regained her strength.
She understood English and could speak it a lit-
tle, but it was easier for her to tell her story to
Mr. Low, who told them:

Her name is Li. Her family, like many, was
starving in China. The drought had shriveled the rice
plants. At one point her mother pounded bricks into
dust which they ate, just to have something in their
stomachs.

They knew they would soon die, including the
baby, so her father said to her, "Of all of my daugh-
ters, you are the smartest. You will survive. You
must help us."

With her consent, her father hired her out to a
rich woman in the city to work as a maid. But her
father had been deceived. Li had really been sold to
the Tong, a group of evil men, who took her and other
girls on a ship to America to work as slaves in bad
places. When the boat arrived, Li was deathly sick
and was allowed to recuperate for three months in
the Sick Room. That's where she learned English.
Then one night, she saw a chance to escape. She
spent the next few months hiding by day, walking
north by night. She was injured, fell and broke her
arm, became sick. She made it to Tacoma, but the
Tongs are still pursuing her. They track down all of

the girls who escape. None make it to freedom. Li hopes she will be the first.

Ty hugged Minus a little tighter as Mr. Low told Li's story. Eva's eyes were wide with awe.

"I believe if you wrote down your adventures, you would have a fascinating book," she told Li. "Such a courageous person."

Li looked at her almost defiantly and spoke in Chinese. Mr. Low translated: *When it is your life, you will do anything you can. You become a fighter. As soon as I recover now, I will continue to Canada. It is only there that I can truly be free.*

***

Slowly Li got stronger. Every day Eva would run home after school to sit with her. Ty and Minus would stop by after they'd visited Mrs. Low and eaten. The highlight of their time together was when Eva read to them. She'd brought many books with her from New York, including Mark Twain's *Tom Sawyer.*

"At home I read three or more hours a day," said Eva. "It was one of my chief pleasures. Often I'd buy some lemon drops, sit in a big chair, suck on the candies and read all afternoon. I may be a writer when I grow up. Or an actress. Perhaps both."

Ty had never read books or heard stories so he could hardly wait to hear what adventure Tom and his friend Huck would have next. He was amazed that when Eva read, he could actually see pictures in his mind about what was happening. When Tom tricked his friends into painting a fence for him, Ty laughed out loud.

"I would like to meet Tom Sawyer someday," Ty said. "He'd be a fun friend."

Eva looked at him curiously. "Tom Sawyer is made up," she said. "Mark Twain made him up."

"They seem so real," Ty said. "And funny."

"I image Mr. Twain probably knew boys like that in real life. Maybe he was like Tom himself."

Li sat up a little more in her bed. "I cannot read," she said. "But Grandmother told me many stories."

Ty's pa certainly didn't tell him stories. What else was out there, Ty wondered, that he had never heard about?

CHAPTER 7: FOUND

A cloth is not woven from a single thread.

Jacob Weisbach swept the floor of his dry goods store calmly and methodically. He enjoyed sweeping. He liked keeping his store tidy and he liked keeping busy. He was an organized man who prided himself on working hard.

He hummed an old German folk song and continued his sweeping. Charles Smith who ran the printing press down the block, pushed open the door.

"Look this over before I run off a hundred copies, will you?" Smith said, waving a poster. "Is it OK?"

Weisbach leaned his broom against the wall and read the text carefully.

"Good!" he said.

Smith nodded, took the poster back and rolled it up. "Hope this meeting convinces people," he said. "We got to make the Chinese leave <u>now</u>. Jacob, it's your job as mayor to make that happen. That's why we voted you in. You promised jobs for everyone. It's not happening."

Weisbach frowned. Was it his fault the economy turned bad this past year? Of course not.

Yet now the bad job market in Tacoma reflected poorly on him. What was he supposed to do?

Well, his top priority continued to get men working in town, American men. That was why the Chinese had to leave. Weisbach himself had come from Germany, but he was now an American citizen. Most of the Chinese legally couldn't become citizens because of the recent Chinese Exclusion Act. Citizens should have first crack at the jobs, shouldn't they? Weisbach didn't hate the Chinese but they just didn't fit in. And they didn't help the town's economy by spending any money. All they did was take. Thus the mayor's goal was to "encourage" them to leave – for their own good. Wouldn't it be better for them to find a place that actually wanted them? Where exactly was that place? He had no idea, just not Tacoma.

"Did you hear they found a sick Chinese girl on the beach last week?" Smith asked, interrupting the mayor's thoughts.

Weisbach nodded.

"What are you going to do about it?" his friend demanded. "It'd set a bad example if she stays here."

Weisbach looked at Smith with irritation. Now he was supposed to get rid of every sick runaway? Getting the established Chinese to leave was hard enough. He sighed. Well, perhaps he should chat with the woman caring for this young girl. He'd use his considerable charm and powers of persuasion. After all, he was the mayor, wasn't he? He could help the woman see the need to let the girl go back to California.

"All right," he said to Smith. "I shall pay her a call. I'll see what I can do."

***

The next afternoon Mrs. Doyle opened her front door to a well-dressed, important-looking gentleman with a full gray beard. He bowed slightly, smiled, and with a German accent, said, "Mrs. Doyle? Allow me to introduce myself, I am Jacob Weisbach, mayor of this wonderful town. How are you this fine day?"

Mrs. Doyle was wary. She'd heard about the mayor. She didn't say anything, just waited.

Mayor Weisbach was unperturbed. "I come as an official representative of our city. I know that you very kindly helped out a poor Chinese girl. So very Christian of you. Unfortunately, now that she has recovered, I must request that she leaves. New Chinese immigrants cannot stay in our town. Jobs are so very hard to come by. Americans must come first. I'm sure you understand."

Mrs. Doyle looked puzzled. "The poor girl is hurt," she said. "I can't throw her out into the street. She would die."

"Not thrown out, no," Mayor Weisbach said patiently, as if speaking to a child. "But it's time to move on. Perhaps she can go back to San Francisco. Many of her people live there."

"She ran away from slavery, did you know that?" asked Mrs. Doyle, her jaw was tightening. "She was kidnapped and taken from her homeland to be a slave in San Francisco until she dies a horrible death. Is that what you want her to return to?"

Mayor Weisbach shook his head sadly. "Yes I heard she was a 'woman of the night.' You know, you cannot trust women of that kind," he said gently. "Their morals are not our morals."

Mrs. Doyle started to turn red with anger.

Then the mayor thoughtfully stroked his beard. "We'll talk more another time. I'm afraid some people in our town are very agitated, and I don't want this poor young woman to get hurt. It's for her own good that she leaves. And yours. Good day, ma'am." He smiled, tipped his hat in farewell and turned to go. He'd set things in motion now. He walked away, feeling quite proud of how he'd handled the situation.

Mrs. Doyle angrily slammed the door shut.

"You're not going to make Li leave, are you?" Eva asked, worried.

Her mother looked like she'd like to slam the door again. "Of course not!" she said sharply. "First of all, she needs us in order to recover. Second of all, I refuse to let bullies tell me what to do."

Mrs. Doyle went back to the parlor, agitated and unhappy, to continue her typing. At the table, she took a few breaths to calm down. Truth be told, she was worried. How could she support them if the mayor made her life difficult? Perhaps it was a mistake to come so far west, as far away from New York City as she could get. Perhaps she should have stayed with her husband, no matter what shape he was in. She'd been desperate! And confident in her abilities to make a new life. Perhaps she was overconfident. Why weren't things ever easy? She needed some good luck once in a while. She took another deep breath. Well, she could feel sorry for herself as much as she wanted, she still had work to do.

She pulled her chair closer to the typewriter, sighed, and began typing.

***

A few days later something horrible happened.

Li had been at Mrs. Doyle's for almost two weeks and was getting stronger daily. That day, Eva was reading *Toby Tyler* to Ty and Li. They were seated around the kitchen table, Minus at Ty's feet. As Eva read, Ty was thinking how fun it would be to have a monkey like Mr. Stubbs. He and Minus could have fun with a monkey.

Suddenly they heard a knock at the front door. Ty could hear Mrs. Doyle opening the door and a man's voice say, "My name is Kaw Chung. I've been told you are keeping my employee here."

"We do not have your employee," Mrs. Doyle told the man.

Ty glanced at Li, frozen at the kitchen table. Her eyes were wide with horror. Who was this man? Ty got up to find out.

At the front door, he saw a slim, well-dressed man standing in front of Mrs. Doyle. He wore a dark silk tunic. His lips were full and wide, his

cheekbones high. His face looked like it was chis-
eled out of some fine wood. His eyes were cold
and arrogant.

"I've been told you have her," said Kaw
Chung. "She must return with me. She is 19
years old. I brought her over from China. She
signed a contract." He held up an official-looking
document.

"No," said Mrs. Doyle. "Absolutely not."

"I have the police here," the man said. He
beckoned and a policeman waiting in the yard
walked up to the house.

"I am Officer DeWitt. This man says you have
his worker," the policeman said. He was tall,
pudgy, and twitchy. He looked uncomfortable,
standing there.

"We are taking care of a Chinese girl," said
Mrs. Doyle. "She is very sick. But she is not this
man's employee."

"He says she is," Officer DeWitt said, his
right eye twitching. "She needs to go with him."

"She is <u>not</u> his employee. But even if she was,
he can't make her come with him," says Mrs.
Doyle. "This is a free country."

"She is in default of a thousand dollar loan to
my company which paid to bring her over here,"
Kaw Chung said. "She has an obligation to work

55

for the company until that debt is paid off. She signed an agreement saying she will work for our company for five years in exchange for her passage. I am here to see that she pays that debt."

"If you send that girl back with him," Mrs. Doyle said to the policemen. "I will make sure you are arrested." Officer DeWitt gulped.

"She comes with me," said the Chinese man, his face bland, his eyes hard.

Officer DeWitt pulled at his collar nervously. "Well, we're taking her into custody and sorting this whole thing out," he said.

"She is not leaving this house. She is sick. If she dies, I will have you arrested for murder," says Mrs. Doyle. "You go sort it out on your own somewhere else."

"Aw come on, now," said Officer DeWitt in a pleading tone. "You're disobeying the law."

"No, you are," said Mrs. Doyle. "She's not moving."

Kaw Chung stared at them with his ice-cold eyes. "I will not leave this town without her," he said to them. "She has a debt. It must be paid."

Office DeWitt gulped a few more times and tugged his collar again. "Well, I'll let her stay here tonight because the chief is out of town," he said. "But tomorrow morning I'm taking her down to the police station. Chief Cooper can sort this out. For now, we'll put a guard outside to make sure she doesn't leave."

When they were gone, Ty and Mrs. Doyle returned to the kitchen. Li was clearly agitated. "That man is a Tong," she said, her voice shaking. "He is bad."

"We won't let you go," said Mrs. Doyle. "But we may need help. I'll talk to Mr. and Mrs. Low."

Li stayed home with Eva, while Mrs. Doyle and Ty hurried to the restaurant.

Mrs. Low, of course, was furious when they told her. Mr. Low just frowned, thinking. He'd been under a lot of stress lately, trying to keep his restaurant going. Was this something he should get involved with? He had to think of his business. He had to support his family.

Mrs. Low, though, had no such conflict.

"Take that girl at once and leave," she said to Mrs. Doyle. "Get her to Canada immediately."

"We can't," Mrs. Doyle said. "They've stationed a guard outside our house.

"Humph," said Mrs. Low. She thought for a bit. "Well, the least we can do is to get a crowd tomorrow to protest this. We can arrange a crowd, can't we, Mr. Low?"

Mr. Low sighed. He could never say no to his wife. "Since only one of us can actually get up and walk throughout the town, I will take arrange a crowd," he said.

Mrs. Low laughed, but they all knew the situation wasn't funny. It was life or death. Ty didn't want to think about Li leaving, forced to return with that evil man to slavery. It couldn't happen, could it? Could people be so cruel? What was going to happen? Ty suddenly realized that having friends could be nerve-wracking. He'd never had to worry about other people before. His only concern had been to escape people's attention, to survive in his own world. Now he saw that having friends – caring about them – could be painful.

***

No one slept well that night.

Early the next morning, Ty and Minus ran down to Eva's house. They were there when Officer DeWitt and Kaw Chung came to get Li. Ty thought Officer DeWitt still looked nervous. Kaw Chung, though, looked as cool and determined as before.

"Come on now," Officer DeWitt said. "The Chief of Police is waiting."

"You will be sorry," said Mrs. Doyle. "You are doing something wrong. This will not end well for you."

Officer DeWitt gulped, twitched, looked nervously at Kaw Chung and said, "She still has to come with me." He reached out to grab Li.

"Don't you dare touch her," Mrs. Doyle said. "We'll all walk with you to the police station. She is still weak. You'll be sorry, mark my words."

Li looked terrified but Mrs. Doyle held her good hand, and Eva and Ty went to her other side, to act as her escorts. They walked ahead of Officer DeWitt and Kaw Chung.

No one talked as they marched downtown.

Outside the station a crowd had already formed. Mr. Low wasn't there, but obviously he had been busy spreading the word. Mrs. Doyle walked forcefully to the front of the crowd. "This poor girl must be released," she told the crowd. "She was kidnapped from her home in China."

Kaw Chung walked up to the front too. "She signed a contract. She will return with me to pay off her debt of one thousand dollars," he said loudly. "In America, people honor their contracts."

"In America, people are free," said Mrs. Doyle, her voice rising so all could hear. Just then Police Chief Cooper, a blustery fellow with a big stomach and a red face, came out of the station. One of Mrs. Doyle's customers had told her that the chief had recently been suspected of taking bribes and being friendly to criminals; he now seemed to be trying very hard to follow the letter of the law.

"Everyone, calm down!" he shouted to the crowd.

"Send the harlot back to San Francisco!" yelled Mrs. Simpson, wife of a banker. A few other people yelled in agreement.

Mrs. Doyle looked at them in shock. "Do you know what you would return her to?" she asked, aghast. "Slavery of the worst kind! The Civil War was fought to end all slavery."

The crowd murmured. Chief Cooper took off his cap and wiped his sweating forehead.

"Well, I'm going to send her back down to San Francisco," he said. "This whole mess belongs down there. We don't have the facts."

"Pontius Pilate!" exclaimed Mrs. Doyle. "You can't wash your hands of this. It'll be your fault when she dies."

"Now Mrs. Doyle," he protested. The crowd was getting angry.

Just then Mr. Low arrived and hurried to the front of the crowd, holding a large sack.

"Stop!" Mr. Low said. "Look! We have collected money to pay her debt." He handed the bag to Police Chief Cooper.

"Mrs. Low came up with an idea as to how we could help this girl," Mr. Low continued. "We passed the hat first among the staff and patrons at my restaurant. Then among other businesses. Finally I went to Little Canton. The men there are saving everything to send home to their families, and yet look at what they gave. We have seven hundred twenty-five dollars total there."

Chief Cooper looked surprised and peered into the bag filled with coins and bills.

Kaw Chung scoffed. "The debt is for one thousand dollars," he sneered. "She owes us that. We cannot get another worker for less than that."

"You mean, you cannot kidnap another girl from the streets of China," said Mrs. Doyle.

Father Hylebos, the Catholic priest in town, stepped forward. "You have to let her go, Charles," he told the police chief. "This man has no claim on her."

Kaw Chung waved an official document. "Right here," he said. "It is a contract."

Ty whispered something to Eva. She clapped her hands with delight.

"But she can't read or write!" Eva shouted. "She's told us that. She's from a small village in China and never went to school. How can she sign a contract if she can't read or write?"

The crowd's murmurs grew to a rumble. That seemed to be all that Chief Cooper needed to hear. He took the sack of money from Mr. Low and handed it to Kaw Chung. "I don't know a lot, but I do know if this case goes to court, it'll cost us all a lot of money and time and agitation," he said. "So you, sir, take this money and get out of here. And don't come back. I will arrest you, sir, if you do."

Mrs. Doyle smiled triumphantly. "Finally!" she said. "You have used common sense."

The police chief waved his hand. "Go on. We're done here. Go home." He looked at the crowd. "That's it, everyone. Leave. I've made up my mind." He went back into the police station. Officer DeWitt looked nervously at the angry crowd and followed his chief.

Kaw Chung, furious, turned and angrily walked away, the sack of money in his hands.

Ty watched him go and wondered if he would try to return. Mrs. Doyle and Eva were smiling with relief and happiness. Was everything ok now? He glanced at Li but she still looked worried. Ty realized she knew that she'd never be totally safe in this country. But at least for the time-being, she was safe, wasn't she? Wasn't she? Ty certainly hoped so.

***

In the days after Li returned home, she seemed to change. She held her head even higher, more proudly, almost defiantly. Her arm was taking a long time to heal, yes, but her spirit was stronger than ever. Her body was regaining its strength too. Every day, she would walk miles around Tacoma. Sometimes Ty, Minus, and Eva would join her. She didn't need them, though. She'd walk and walk, up and down the hills, down on the waterfront, through the woods. She had to walk. She'd been on that ship for too long. She'd been in the sick room in San Francisco for too long. She'd been recuperating in Tacoma, in bed, for too long. Now she wanted to walk, just as she had walked from San Francisco to Tacoma.

Had her family ever found out they had been tricked and she had been sent to America? She had no idea. She tried to remember if she'd even heard of America before she was kidnapped. Her life had been small, contained, up until she left home. Her days revolved around her family, her village, their little hut, their daily work in the rice fields, their daily struggle to feed the family. If Li had stayed at home, she soon would have been married and left her family. She left earlier, that's all, and she went farther, across the ocean to America.

As Li walked and thought about these things, she set her jaw a little harder. She was determined. Her broken arm meant she must stay in Tacoma for now. Would her arm ever heal? The doctor said she might not ever be able to straighten it. She knew it was wise to stay until she could work again. It'd be hard enough to find work, even when she was healthy. To find work with a broken arm would be impossible.

She was thankful to Mrs. Doyle for allowing her to live with her. It would not be in vain. She would make it to Canada and thrive. She would survive. But she needed a plan.

Learning to read and write and speak better English would be her first goal. She could do that as she recovered. Learning this might ensure survival. On the ship coming to America she realized that the difference between life and death, slavery or freedom, was making an extra effort, never relaxing, always thinking, always pushing forward. She'd have time to rest when she was older. Now she must be always ready, always alert, always learning. She was determined.

CHAPTER 8: TY IS CIVILIZED

A speck on a jade stone
can't obscure its brilliance.

One Saturday morning when Li had already left to walk down on the waterfront, Ty and Minus stopped by Eva's house, ready for a day of adventure.

Ty liked going to the Doyles' house. The whole atmosphere seemed so different than his own. At Eva's, the floors were clean, the furniture was dusted, the smell of freshly baked bread often lingered in the air. Sometimes Ty sensed that Mrs. Doyle was busy, sometimes overwhelmed. Sometimes she couldn't talk to him for long because she had to type or shop for groceries or cook or wash clothes. Still, more than anything, Ty could feel that people liked each other in that home. Home. That's what it was, he thought, a true home.

His house didn't feel like a home. Nobody cleaned or cooked much. The floors were filthy. The kitchen table was cluttered with dirty plates and crusty pans. Ty had never seen a broom in the house. He slept by the kitchen stove during the winter, but if his brothers or pa came in to eat, he'd slip out to the barn to get away from their bullying. Pa didn't seem to like any of his sons, but he tolerated Sam and Fred, probably because they could defend themselves now. When the three of them started drinking, well, Ty couldn't be anywhere close. They delighted in pushing him around and taunting him.

Eva's house was different. Best of all, he could always count on Eva and Mrs. Doyle to offer him some food.

On that Saturday morning, Eva gave him some oatmeal and fried eggs and watched him eat. When he finished, she smiled and said, "Tyrus Ritter, the time has come for you to join the human race."

What? He looked at her in surprise. What did she mean by that?

"You have not been trained in manners," said Eva. "For your own good, you need to learn social etiquette."

Well, fine. Ty knew he was stupid in many areas. His pa and his brothers lived like critters of the barnyard – dirty, stinky, sloppy. Maybe if his ma had lived, she would have taught them how to act in polite society. Had his ma cared about such things? Well, maybe it was time for him to learn.

"First thing," said Eva. "You must wash. You're filthy. Your face, your hands, your clothes are extremely dirty. I don't mind it so much because I can look past the dirt and see the valuable diamond hidden underneath, but other people won't be able to get past your grime. Come look in the mirror and see for yourself."

Mirror? Ty's pa and brothers used a cracked, murky one when they bothered to shave. But Ty didn't need to shave and never bother looking into it.

Eva led Ty to a long mirror in the hallway. "Tyrus Ritter, I would like to introduce you to Tyrus Ritter," said Eva, pointing to the mirror. Ty looked into it and for the first time in his life saw his whole reflection.

At first glance he thought the fellow looking at him was a street urchin. He saw a boy with long, ragged, matted brown hair, grimy face, torn and dirty overalls, and ripped shirt. His bare feet were crusted in dirt as well. Then he looked into his own eyes. The eyes that met his were brown and intelligent. That startled him, that he had intelligent eyes. Then, embarrassed, he looked away.

"First things first," said Eva, regarding him closely. "You definitely need a bath, but why take a bath if you don't have clean clothes? Do you have anything else to wear?"

Ty nodded. "But they are worse than these," he said.

Eva frowned. This was a predicament. Hmmm. Then her face lit up. "My mother can sew. She's tried to teach me, but I detest it. Still, if I try to sew you something, Mother will soon try to help me. That way you'll get clothes that actually look decent. In the meantime, though, there are other areas you can improve on."

Ty suddenly got the sinking feeling that this was going to be a long and painful process.

"At the very least you can wash your hands," Eva said, leading him to the kitchen sink where water was piped in from a nearby spring. Ty was impressed since he always had to go outside to pump water at his house. Ty took the bar of soap and scrubbed.

When he was done, he showed Eva. She carefully examined his hands. "Passable," she said. "Now let's work on table manners."

Ty perked up. Did that mean more food?

Eva sat him down at the table and set out some bread and butter. "What do you do now?" she asked, playing the role of a stern teacher.

Eat! He stood up, grabbed the bread, ripped off a big chunk and stuffed it in his mouth. He gave it a couple chews, then lunged to get another piece as he swallowed.

"No, no, no!" Eva said.

Ty looked at her, bewildered. What could be wrong about eating?

"Never stand," said Eva. "Sit with both feet on the ground and at the edge of your seat. Put your napkin in your lap. If you need something you can't reach, ask someone to please pass it."

Seemed like a waste of words to Ty, but he wanted to learn, so he pointed to the bread and said, "Pass it."

"<u>Please</u> pass the bread and butter."

"Please," said Ty.

Eva rolled her eyes and passed them to him. He looked at her for further instruction. "Slice the bread and place it on your plate," Eva said. "Put a slice of butter on your plate, then spread a bit of the butter onto the bread. Eat one bite at a time. Chew, swallow. Then take another bite."

Ty looked at her incredulously. This would take forever!

"People take time with their food," Eva explained. "They enjoy eating."

Ty had never thought about enjoying food. His stomach ached to be filled. Food didn't taste good or bad, it just filled that ache.

"Take your napkin," said Eva, holding up her cloth. "And wipe your face if you feel food or crumbs on it. Then you put it in your lap to catch any crumbs or spills so you don't get your clothes dirty … although in your current state, it wouldn't matter."

Ty was overwhelmed with how complicated this business of manners was. He was still hungry, and he really wanted more of that bread. When Eva left to get the tea, he stood up, reached for the bread, and crammed a big piece into his mouth. He only had so much patience. Minus had been sleeping at his feet all of this time, so Ty ripped off a piece for him. He made Minus sit before he gave him the treat, figuring he might as well teach the dog some manners too.

***

Eva had to admit, civilizing Ty was a challenge. "You're like Romulus and Remus, two boys raised by wolves," she said. "They couldn't be harder than this. This will be a long-term project."

In the parlor of Eva's house was an old upright piano which had come with the house. One day when Ty came to visit, Mrs. Doyle was at the piano, playing from some sheet music. Li and Eva were seated on the couch, sipping tea and listening.

Ty was fascinated. Of course, he'd seen people play the piano, but never up close. He immediately went over to watch Mrs. Doyle's fingers move across the keyboard. She noticed him watching her.

"You'd find this interesting, Ty, because music is mathematical," she said. "Music is all about vibrations. Eight notes apart is an octave. From middle C to high C, the vibrations are exactly doubled. It's fascinating."

Ty looked at the notes on the page, and then he closed his eyes and listened to Mrs. Doyle play. What was it about music that made him feel the way it did? That reached deep inside of him? Wouldn't it be wonderful to be able to make music like that?

Eva came over then and sang as her mother played.

I am bound for the promised land, bound for the promised land.

Oh, who will come and go with me?

I am bound for the promised land.

Her voice was pure and clear, sweet even. Something about her singing touched Ty in a way he had never felt before. He wiped his eyes quickly.

Eva looked up just then and knew immediately he wasn't crying sad tears. "Wait here," she said. "I have something for you." She ran back to her room and came back with an object wrapped in tissue paper.

"A gift for you," she told Ty. "Here." And she handed it to him.

He opened it and saw a metal object about three inches long.

"It's a harmonica," Eva said. "You blow into it, and music will come out. Try it." Ty gently blew into the harmonica. Notes did come out!

"Now try sucking in," said Eva. Ty did, and the notes were different.

"When you blow to the right, higher notes will come out. Blow to the left, and lower notes will," said Eva. "I never play it. It's yours."

Ty couldn't remember ever having been given a gift before. He felt overwhelmed with Eva's generosity. The possibilities of this little instrument were thrilling to him. Imagine! He could make music anytime, anywhere.

"Thank you," he said, his eyes focused on the gift. "I better go now."

"Yes, experiment with it," said Eva. She knew him well.

He ran outside, up the hill, with Minus at his side, to the woods where he could experiment and figure out this harmonica. At first Minus was interested in the sounds coming from his master, but the dog quickly got bored and ran off to chase squirrels. Ty was not a boy who bored easily once he had his mind set on mastering something. By the end of that day, he could play "Mary Had a Little Lamb."

From then on, Ty could always be found with his harmonica in his pocket, that is, if he wasn't actually playing it. He couldn't play at school, and he knew better than to play it for his pa or his brothers. They'd either laugh at him or take the harmonica away. He couldn't bear to have it taken away.

His song repertoire grew as he discovered other tunes to play. He hadn't grown up with any music, but Mrs. Doyle played songs for him on the piano, if she had time. Sometimes Eva would sing him songs, and he tried to copy them on his harmonica.

Often he was impatient sitting in school when he really wanted to be playing new songs.

When he felt ready, Ty took the harmonica to the restaurant to play for Mrs. Low. She smiled to see the earnest young boy, concentrating so hard to play melodies on his little instrument.

"Ah, music," she said. "'He who loves music learns to soothe his own sorrows.'"

After he'd left, Mrs. Low thought how much she would like a son like Ty. Perhaps her baby will be a boy. Perhaps someday her own son will run into her room to show her a discovery he'd made or an instrument he'd learned. On the other hand, she'd certainly enjoy having a girl. Perhaps her daughter would learn chess from her. What, she wondered, was going to happen? In a year from now, would they have a child? Or would their hearts once again be broken. Time would tell. As the proverb said, "Don't try to make predictions – especially those concerning the future."

***

As Ty's daily etiquette lessons progressed, Eva, with her mother's help (or was it her mother with a tiny bit of help from Eva?) sewed Ty a pair of pants and a shirt. When they were finished, Eva said, "Haircut and bath now. It's time."

Ty didn't recollect ever having taken a bath. He'd gotten wet in Puget Sound, of course, when he'd splash about, but filling a tub with hot water and scrubbing himself with soap? Never. And Eva's house had a separate room for the tub. Amazing.

He enjoyed his first bath enormously. To sit in a tub of deliciously warm water, all by himself, was heaven. Outside the bathroom he could hear Minus whining and Eva puttering around. He should have brought his harmonica. Playing in the tub would have made the bath perfect.

And when he emerged from the room, clean, dry, with brand new clothes, Eva was impressed. "Now all you need is a haircut and you'll be fit for society," she declared.

She took out a big pair of scissors from Mrs. Doyle's sewing basket and set to work. When he finally looked into the long mirror again, he couldn't help but grin at his new image. What would the kids at school say when they saw him? Ty had never felt so proud.

One thing he hadn't counted on, though, was his brothers' reactions back home. As he happily walked up to the house that afternoon in his new clothes and haircut, his brothers were pumping a bucket of water.

"Well look at that!" hooted Fred. "Mr. Fancy Pants come a'calling!"

"Didn't you forget your name is Dirt?" asked Sam. He grabbed Ty and shoved him to the ground. Fred, laughing, rubbed dirt into his hair and then helped him up. Ty dusted himself off. They hadn't done any damage. His brothers couldn't ruin his happy mood.

"Look Pa," said Ty proudly when his pa came home later. "I got new clothes." But his pa was in a dark mood and hardly looked at him. Instead, he fried up some eggs, ate, and went into his bedroom.

When Ty went to bed that night, he folded his clothes as neatly as he could and put them on the kitchen chair. Soon it would be warm enough for him to sleep out in the barn with Minus. He looked forward to that. He went to sleep by the stove, feeling happy and proud.

The next morning, though, when he woke up, he went to the chair to get his new clothes. The chair was empty, the clothes were gone. Ty looked everywhere. He started to get shaky inside, he was so angry. He found his old dirty overalls and a ripped shirt outgrown by Fred and put them on. Hot with anger, he ran upstairs to his brothers' attic room. "What did you do with my clothes," he demanded.

Fred stirred in his bed. "Pa took them," he mumbled. "Go away."

Furious, Ty ran back down the stairs and into his pa's room. "Where are my clothes?" He'd hardly ever gone into that room before, certainly never in anger.

His pa was snoring in bed. "Where are my clothes?" Ty asked, louder.

"Get outta here," his pa said into his pillow, not even opening his eyes. Ty could smell the odor of stale beer.

"I want my clothes," Ty insisted stubbornly. "They're mine."

"Johnnie at the Swan gave me four beers for 'em," said his pa. "He has a kid your size. You don't need no fancy clothes."

"They were mine," said Ty, his voice trembling. "You had no right."

Pa sat up, his eyes red, his hair sticking up. "I'll show you who got the right," he snarled. He threw a tin mug towards Ty, but it missed him and hit the door. "Get the hell out of here."

Suddenly Ty felt sick to his stomach. What would he tell Eva and Mrs. Doyle? They'd worked so hard. He felt like crying.

He went out to the barn where Minus waited to be let out. Even his dog couldn't cheer him up. "Come on," Ty told Minus. "We better tell Eva."

***

When Eva opened the door, she took one look at her friend and saw that he was dressed in his old, dirty clothes, looking as miserable as she'd ever seen him. "What happened?" she asked. "Are you all right?"

"He took my clothes," Ty said in a shaky voice. "He traded 'em for beer. They're gone." And he sat down on the front step and sobbed, right in front of her. He never cried anymore. But he just couldn't help it. Minus couldn't stand the sound of his master crying. He whined and tried to jump up on him.

"Hey, hey, hey," said Eva, trying to calm both her friend and his dog. "They're just clothes. We can make more, even better ones. Those were just practice."

"He'll take those too," said Ty and buried his face in his hands.

Eva patted his head. "Ah, but we are smarter than he is. You'll have a set of clothes that you'll keep here. Maybe two sets. You wear your old clothes at home and then change here. You'll see, it'll be all right."

Ty sobbed until he was all sobbed out. He wiped his eyes and then his nose with his dirty shirt sleeve. Eva's words comforted him a little.

"If you keep calm and plan, you can figure out a way to go around obstacles," she said. "You just have to be smarter than the opposition."

Ty stroked his dog's head until he felt better. Then he stood up. It was clear what he had to do. "I want to learn to read," he said.

"Now?" asked Eva, surprised.

"If I'm going to be smarter than Pa is, I got to learn to read." He looked at Eva with great determination.

"Well, come on inside," said Eva. "Let's start."
***
Mrs. Doyle was puzzled by Ty's not being able to read.

"I don't understand it," she said. "Obviously you're very smart. But why is reading so hard?"

"Maybe," Ty said, "I'm just half-smart. Only smart with numbers. Letters just get all mixed up. They don't make sense."

"Hmmm," said Mrs. Doyle, frowning as she thought. "We have to be clever here. Maybe try something different."

Ty waited while she thought. Minus sat patiently at his feet.

Mrs. Doyle had a stack of work to do, many pages to type. She'd been putting off trying to teach Ty because she'd been so busy, and frankly, she had no idea how to help him. She looked at his hopeful, expectant face and her heart sank. Her daughter thought she could do anything. Well, she couldn't. And teach a boy who couldn't learn how to read? She sighed and looked into the parlor where she could see her desk and the stack of work to be done. Sometimes she thought buying a typewriter had been a shortsighted idea. Going as far away from New York as she could probably also was naïve. She sighed and looked at Ty. Almost against her will, an idea formulated in her mind.

"Ty," Mrs. Doyle said. "Have you ever seen a typewriter?"

He had, from afar. He loved machines and had been itching to examine her writing machine, but he'd been too shy to ask about it. It seemed magical. You could hit a key which would make a lever pop up and print a letter on a page. Amazing.

"Come into the parlor," Mrs. Doyle said. She took the shawl that she used as a dust cover off the typewriter. "Look, I will now type the letter 'a'."

With her forefinger, she struck the letter on the keyboard. There, on the white piece of paper, the letter 'a' appeared. "Now you try it ... the letter 'a'."

Ty pushed down the key she pointed to tentatively. No mark was made.

"Strike it harder," Mrs. Doyle said.

He whammed his forefinger on the letter 'a' hard. There! On the page. He had made the letter 'a.' It looked like a stubby snail.

"Do it again. Do it several times."

Ty grinned and hit the key over and over. 'a.' 'a.' 'a.'

"Now what letter is that?" asked Mrs. Doyle.

"a," said Ty.

Mrs. Doyle turned Ty with his back to the typewriter, then she moved it to a slightly new position. Then she turned Ty back. "Find the letter 'a' now," she said.

He grinned again. Of course he knew what it looked like: the stubby snail. He found the key and hit it. Again and again and again and again.

" a...a...a...a...a"

Mrs. Doyle smiled at him. "Go ahead, look inside the typewriter. I know you want to figure it out."

Even though she needed to start work, she knew Ty needed time on his own with the machine. The kitchen needed cleaning, she thought, so she and Eva left Ty alone to examine, experiment and enjoy the typewriter.

Li came into the room as Ty was figuring out exactly how the machine operated. "I must learn to read and write too," she said. "You teach me?"

Ty blushed. "I can't yet," he said.

Li looked wistful. "I can't ask Mrs. Doyle. She has done too much already."

Ty hit the 'a' key several times and thought. Then he said, "Maybe Mrs. Low can help you. She's real smart."

Later that afternoon he brought Li over to the restaurant.

"Will you help her to learn reading and writing?" Ty asked Mrs. Low.

Mrs. Low looked at the slight young girl standing before her. "I will teach you, but only if you want to learn both English and Chinese. You ought to know how to read and write your native language. Reading will change your life. And as the proverb says, 'A book is like a garden carried in the pocket.'"

"I want to learn everything," said Li. "I am hungry to learn."

"Good. I like you. I also like that you have big feet like mine," said Mrs. Low. "We will begin at once. I will write down ancient Chinese proverbs in both Chinese and English. You will learn all my wisdom. As they say, 'The old horse knows the way.'"

After they left that afternoon, Mrs. Low had something new to think about. In the past month, when she showed Ty a move in chess, she watched his eyes. A spark behind his eyes flickered when he understood something. Her sharp eyes saw that. She wanted to get that spark to flicker in the girl's eyes too. She relished the challenge. "My time on this couch might be useful to someone," she thought. She certainly hoped it was useful to her baby.

CHAPTER 9: A NEW ADDITION

If heaven above lets fall a plum,
open your mouth.

Ever since his pa had stolen his good clothes, Ty hated being in his house. School took up most of the day, and he tried to be out exploring as much as he could. Still, a boy has to rest his head somewhere. He had to sleep in the kitchen, by the stove, hoping Pa and his brothers would ignore him.

Whenever Mrs. Doyle had a few extra minutes, even though she was often exhausted, she worked on sewing Ty another pair of pants and shirt to keep at her house. Eva mended and washed his old clothes so they were presentable.

"We'll keep your good set of clothes here for special occasions," Mrs. Doyle said. We don't want your father to see them. Your old clothes will be fine for now."

Finally, at the end of May, the weather was warm enough for him to sleep out in the barn. He decided to make the drafty, old building into his own little home. Nobody went out there, not since they'd gotten rid of the animals. Why not fix it up a little?

Ty stood at the barn door one Saturday morning and looked inside. Light streamed through the cracks in the sides and ceiling. Planks had been put down in a rough fashion to make a floor. Hay and dirt covered the planks. A blanket for Minus lay in the middle of the barn. Old hay bales were stacked here and there. Lumber, probably left over from building the house and barn, was tossed randomly around. A broken ladder lay in a corner. A work bench had collapsed in another one. Some wooden crates were piled next to the work bench. Ty heard a noise and saw a mouse disappear into some of the hay. Minus didn't seem to care but Ty did. He didn't mind mice and rats in the woods, but he didn't want to share a bedroom with them. What if one ran over him when he slept?

When he told Eva that later, she said, "The solution is obvious. You need a cat."

Ty looked at her, puzzled. He had a dog. Didn't dogs and cats fight? And how could he take care of a cat?

"Cats take care of themselves," explained Eva. "They eat all sorts of things – rats, mice, birds, and even fish, if they can catch them. They're independent creatures and very helpful if you have an abundance of rodents."

"I don't know how to get a cat," said Ty.

"I'll find you one," said Eva. And within a day, she had. The next afternoon she came up to his house, and in her arms, wrapped up in a big towel, she held a twisting, scrawny, furious black cat. When she let him out of the towel, he glared at Eva, turned his back to her, and started licking his paw in obvious contempt of her.

Minus, curious and eager, ran up to inspect the cat. The cat arched his back and hissed so fiercely Minus ran behind Ty for protection.

"Isn't he wonderful," said Eva, looking with pride at the cat. "I want you to call him Angel, because he will be your barn angel."

Ty was not a boy who laughed much, but seeing the cat and hearing that name, he burst out with a short, rusty-sounding guffaw. The mangy black cat looked the exact opposite of an angel. He was so skinny his backbone could be seen, patches of black fur were missing, and he had a crooked tail and chewed up ear. One eye was closed, probably from a recent fight with some other cat.

"Angel has been living around the black-smith's house," said Eva. "But the blacksmith said he was going to shoot him. I saved him. Now you will give him a home."

Ty reached down to pet the pathetic-looking cat. In a quick second, the cat reached out its claws and scratched Ty's hand. Ow! Bewildered, Ty looked up at Eva. She shrugged, not concerned.

"He's ill-tempered and cantankerous," she said. "But you don't need another animal to love, you have Minus. You want one to work for you."

But, despite the red scratch on his hand, Ty couldn't help himself: the arrogant fierceness and independence of the rough-looking cat made Ty start to love him.

"If you give cats a little food now and then, they'll realize this is home," said Eva. "I brought food for just that purpose." She unwrapped several pieces of chicken, and the half-starved cat gobbled them down in just a few seconds. Then, as full as he'd probably ever been in his short life, he turned around several times on the old towel Eva set down in the barn floor, and promptly went to sleep.

And that was how Ty acquired his second pet. It was also how Ty kept his new sleeping space free of mice and rats.

Ty enjoyed the challenge of setting up a cor-ner of the barn to be his bedroom. He took the old wooden fruit crate to use as a shelf. In the shelf he put his treasures, items that he'd found exploring the woods and waterfront: an old blue bottle that had washed up on the waterfront shore, a shimmery black and green feather, a pale blue shell of a bird egg, a smooth, round, tan stone. He took his blanket from the house and spread it on the old hay. He arranged some of the items he found in the barn – an old wooden wagon wheel, a battered milking stool, and part of a barrel, to divide his room from the rest of the barn.

Sometimes he got cold sleeping in the drafty barn, but he always had Minus close by to hug for warmth. Hearing his dog snore lightly and being able to stroke his coarse fur whenever he woke up in the middle of the night, comforted him. Angel slept at his feet, just out of reach. If Ty twisted so he could pet the cat, he soon learned he could stroke him three times, no more. At the fourth petting, Angel would irrita-bly turn and bite Ty's hand, not enough to break the skin but enough to let Ty know he'd had enough. Sometimes, though, Angel allowed Ty to rest his hand on his back, and then Ty would be rewarded by a low, vibrating purr. It was a small victory, but one that pleased Ty greatly.

Minus learned quickly to stay clear of the cat. Angel hissed and swatted at the dog anytime he got near, and Ty was pretty sure if they ever got into a fight, the ornery cat would win easily over the sweet-tempered dog.

Angel immediately accepted that this was his new home. He didn't act grateful, he just took it as his due. Once in a while, he'd come over to Ty and allow his ears or his back, right above the tail, to be scratched. Still Ty figured the cat liked him. Ty made sure his critters had fresh water, and he'd sometimes withheld a scrap or two from Minus to feed Angel. Mostly, though, the cat hunted and fed himself.

One of the best things about staying in the barn was that Ty didn't have to see his pa or his brothers very often. Occasionally he'd see one or another going to the outhouse or pumping water. Sometimes, before or after school, Ty would go to the kitchen to find something to eat. Ty could hear his pa yelling now and then. Pa wasn't working these days and was even more surly than usual.

"It's the fault of them damn Chinese," growled Pa one day when Ty was in the kitchen. "They're taking any jobs I could do."

Ty knew better than to say anything. Arguing with Pa would only result in a whack alongside the head. Ty's brothers came into the kitchen just then.

"We hate them too," said Sam, yawning and scratching his belly. "They look funny. Why do they have long hair?"

"We'll get rid of 'em, mark my words," said Pa. "It's our right to work here, not them foreigners."

Ty left the kitchen and went out to the barn. Hearing that ugly talk made him feel shaky inside. He hoped his pa and brothers wouldn't do anything, ever, to hurt his friends.

***

One late afternoon when Ty and Minus got home from school, after visiting Mrs. Low and getting a reading lesson from Mrs. Doyle, he was puzzled to see that the door to the barn was ajar. He always made sure to close it because he didn't want anyone to just wander in, including his brothers or more rodents. Nervously, he pushed the door open wider, took a step inside and then stopped.

Someone had been in there. Everything was wrecked. His brothers. It was the work of his brothers, he just knew it.

They'd kicked over his crate shelf and broken it. They'd slashed his blanket with a knife. They'd flung the wagon wheel across the barn and had smashed the milking stool. Ty could imagine his brothers laughing as they did their damage.

He looked around. Angel! Where was Angel? Did they hurt his cat? Ty looked everywhere in the barn. Angel wasn't there. His brothers wouldn't stoop that low would they, to hurt a cat? Maybe Angel was out exploring or hunting. Perhaps Ty was worrying for no reason. Angel always came back to the barn to sleep for the night. Ty waited.

When the cat didn't come home that night, Ty knew his brothers had done something to him. Would they be so heartless as to kill him? Would they think it was funny to throw him in a stream? Feed him to a bear? He had a horrible feeling that his brothers were capable of most anything. He had to find his cat.

Ty took a lantern that he kept in the barn and ventured into the darkness of the woods. Minus ran right next to him.

"Angel? Here Cat," Ty called. Normally he hated being in the woods at night. He felt too small, too vulnerable in the immense blackness. A lantern only gave out a small amount of light. Anything could be lurking. His fear didn't matter now. He had to find Angel. Minus was right beside him, giving him courage. The dog seemed to know what his master was looking for. He ran off, then checked back with Ty, then ran off again.

Suddenly, from the darkness, Ty heard Minus barking. Holding his lantern high, Ty tried to find where his dog was. There, under a tree, looking up, was Minus, barking, excited and intent. Ty held the lantern up higher to see a burlap bag, tied tightly to a low tree limb. "Rrrreow," wailed the bag. Ty took out his pocket knife and with one hand, he supported the bag, and with the other he cut the rope that tied it to the limb.

Once he got the bag down, he untied it and out flew his cat, furious at having been captive and uncomfortable for hours. Angel, with great irritation, shook himself and then angrily walked around in the lantern's pool of light.

"Let's go home," whispered Ty. He scooped up the unwilling cat and set off with the lantern in one hand and the squirming cat under his other arm. Minus stayed close to them all the way home.

Ty didn't let the cat go until they were safely inside the barn. "I didn't want you to get lost back there," Ty told him after he'd set him down. The cat didn't even bother to look at him. He angrily stalked around the barn for a minute, then found Ty's blanket and, disgusted, curled up as if trying to forget the whole nightmare.

As Ty tried to go to sleep that night, he wondered why his brothers had been so mean. Did they think this was funny? Did they goad each other on? Sam was meaner than Fred, but Fred must have gone along with it. How could they have done such things?

"I'm never going to be mean," Ty decided. "Not ever." As he drifted off to sleep, he reached out to touch Minus to his left side. Then he bent to reach Angel who had already curled up at his feet. Ty rested his hand on the cat's back, and after a few seconds, was rewarded by the most beautiful sound in the world: the low, soft rumble of a purr.

CHAPTER 10: SMUGGLERS

***If evil was placed like discs on a string,
the string would be always be full.***

Ty took special care after that to make sure that Minus and Angel were never vulnerable to his brothers' tormenting again. When he told Mrs. Low what they'd done, she had Mr. Low look in her desk drawer and take out an old padlock and key.

"This is a railroad padlock," Mrs. Low said. "The rail workers needed to use it to protect all of their equipment when they were setting tracks across country. We traded a wonderful dinner in our restaurant for it. Now it is yours. Keep this key around your neck, and padlock the barn door when you leave. We must outsmart people who wish to do us harm."

His brothers never mentioned what they'd done to the barn or Angel, and probably because of the padlock, they never bothered the barn again.

***

Summer vacation came early that year. "Today is the last day of school," announced Miss Shaw unexpectantly one Friday. "The citizens of

Tacoma did not pay their taxes, thus the teachers cannot get paid and thus the school year is over. Enjoy your summer. I know I will." With a wave of her hand, she released her class from the confines of school and into the glorious freedom of summer.

Vacation was always bliss to Ty. This year, he looked forward to spending it at the Doyles' house, learning to read, and exploring the countryside with Minus. He wasn't a boy for words. He'd never really talked much, but now he often talked to the scruffy three-legged dog by his side. Minus always looked at him like he made sense.

"The mountain is out," he told Minus on the first day of vacation as they were walking down the hill to Eva's house. He stopped to look at Mount Rainier which seemed to hover in the air, over the skyline, in the distance. Sometimes the mountain was completely obscured by clouds, so it was always a treat when any part of it could be seen.

Eva was waiting for them, and they all headed down to the waterfront. "Tacoma is a young town, compared to New York City," said Eva as they walked. Ty hadn't heard of New York City before he met Eva. There was much, it seemed, that he'd never heard of.

"What is New York City like?" he asked.

This seemed to be the very question that Eva was waiting for. "New York City!" exclaimed Eva. "It's crowded, it's bustling, it's always on the go. It's wonderful. You step out of your house, and just walking a block is an adventure. Sights, smells, sounds. Plays and concerts. Museums and restaurants. And people! Why you could just fill your days looking at all the different people, each with a different story."

Ty thought how wonderful those sights must be. Maybe when he grew to be a man, he could travel to New York and see them for himself. He'd never thought about becoming a grown-up. Up until now, it was all he could do to think about making it through the day. But with Eva around, things were different. She knew about the world. She thought about the future. For the first time in his life, he realized that he wouldn't always be the little runt that his pa and brothers could tease and hit. Maybe someday he'd be even bigger and stronger than they were. He shook his head at the thought. It seemed almost impossible now, but maybe....

"This is a good town too," Ty said to Eva. They were on the waterfront now. The water glistened and seagulls swooped.

Eva stopped to look out at the water and the mountain range beyond. "On a sunny day, this must be one of the most beautiful spots in the world," she declared. "New York can't hold a candle to this beauty."

The water lapped gently at the shore. Eva and Ty walked and walked, while Minus ran and ran.

It was Ty's turn now to show Eva a thing or two. For a lonely boy, the northwest landscape had been a playground. He knew the waterfront well, just as he knew many paths through the woods. He turned over large pieces of driftwood that had washed up on the pebbly sand, and they watched little sand crabs scurry away to find new shelter. He pointed out a huge bird's nest that had been in one of the trees, probably for years. Then he showed Eva how to skip a rock.

"First you need to find a flat, round rock," he instructed her. He picked up one that fitted nicely into his hand. He reared his arm back and with a practiced flick of his wrist, sent the rock skipping four times over the water.

"How did you do that?" asked Eva, impressed.

He demonstrated the technique, and after a few tries, she was able to skip a rock once or twice. Minus tried to chase the stones they skipped and plunged happily into the water time after time.

As they walked along the waterfront, Eva suddenly became very quiet. Ty looked over at her with curiosity. Being quiet wasn't like her.

Suddenly she stopped and looked at him, her eyes serious. "I want to tell you about my father," she said. Ty had wondered about him, but Eva never brought him up and he never wanted to pry.

"We lived in New York City," she said, looking out at the water. "My father was a successful surgeon. We went to concerts, the theater, museums. We dined at fancy restaurants. But then…."

She looked down for a second, and Ty saw an odd expression flash over her face. Was it a look of shame? He looked at her, puzzled.

"My father started using opium," she said.

"What is that?" asked Ty.

"A drug. It is not illegal but it is horribly addictive. But he didn't know. He saw that it had potential to take away his patients' pain. He didn't know the risks and so experimented on himself. He learned a lot about it as a painkiller, but…well…he couldn't stop."

"What happened?" Ty asked.

"Mother asked him over and over to stop or to get help. She begged and cried. I'd never seen my mother cry before. She said he would lose his license to practice. He was not himself. She said that he would kill someone or injure them when he was operating. Addiction must be horrible because he wanted to stop but he just couldn't. He's a really good man." She looked at Ty desperately as if begging him to understand. Once again, Ty didn't know what to say.

"Finally, Mother said we had no choice. Leaving him might shake him up into getting help. Or stopping. We left in the middle of the night. I wrote him a letter once we got here. I didn't tell Mother. I begged him to come to us. I miss him so much. We haven't heard from him. Sometimes I hear Mother crying at night."

The two walked in silence, thinking about Eva's father. Ty wondered if he would ever know the words to comfort someone or give them hope. For now, though, he didn't know what to say and so let Eva think her thoughts.

As they rounded an unfamiliar bend, they saw something odd: a heavy-set Indian woman with a shawl wrapped around her shoulders was tending a fire on the beach.

"Why does she have a fire on this warm afternoon?" asked Eva. "She's not cooking anything."

Minus happily ran up to the woman and Eva, friendly as ever, waved and called out "Hello!"

The woman looked at them, alarmed. "Go away," she said. "Go away." Minus started barking.

"That's a strange greeting," said Eva, puzzled. "Why should we go away?"

The woman shook her head fiercely. "Take your dog and go!" Then she looked out to the water. There, in the distance, a boat was coming towards them.

The woman ran in front of the fire and started waving her shawl at the boat.

"What are you doing?" asked Eva.

"Go away," the woman said again. Then she turned to stare at Eva and Ty. "How old are you?" she asked them abruptly.

Eva didn't answer her because her tone was so rude, but Ty was used to doing what he was asked.

"Eleven," he said.

The woman stared at them for a few more seconds, sizing them up. "You are harmless," she said, more to herself than them. "Just children." She walked behind the fire, put her shawl back around her shoulders, and kept looking out to the water. The boat came closer and closer.

"My curiosity has been piqued. I'm not leaving until I see who's on that little ship," said Eva. That was fine by Ty. And so they waited.

In twenty minutes, the boat sailed into the little inlet next to where they stood. The woman went over to move brush away, and to their surprise, Eva and Ty saw that she had uncovered a little dock.

A burly man with a wild black beard was standing on the boat's deck. He threw down a gangplank and angrily strode across it.

"Wife!" he shouted in a fury. "Why were you waving the shawl? I just about dumped the cargo."

"Look," the woman said, jerking her head towards Eva and Ty. "But they are just children and a dog. It is safe."

The big man glared at the children. "They better be safe," he muttered. Then he turned and yelled to someone on the boat. "OK, Jensen, bring the cargo here."

In a few minutes a scrawny little man came into view. Behind him was a line of Chinese men, all tied together with a rope.

"Bring 'em over here," the big man bellowed to Jensen. The little man led the Chinese men over the gangplank.

The men looked exhausted and weak as they staggered onto the beach. One man's knees buckled, and the man behind him caught him as he went down.

"Mr. Ure, he needs water," the man who caught him said. "And food. We haven't had anything to eat or drink."

"Not my business," said the big man who obviously was Mr. Ure. He walked over to the line of men. "Someone will be by soon to pick you up. It's not our job to feed you. They'd have to pay us more. I'm only getting $200 a head."

He looked at his wife. "We're leaving now," he said. "Get in the boat. Come on, Jensen."

"Shall I untie 'em?" Jensen asked.

"Naw," said Mr. Ure. "We gotta go." And motioning for his wife to follow, he headed to the boat and walked up the gangplank. Jensen covered up the dock, boarded the boat and pulled up the gangplank.

Eva and Ty watched the boat chug off, back into the Puget Sound. Then they turned to look at the Chinese men. There were twelve of them.

Twelve times $200 equals $2400. Mr. Ure made $2400 from smuggling those men. A fortune!

Eva ran over to the men, and Ty shyly followed. Minus trotted over as well.

"Hello," said Eva, smiling her most gracious, welcoming smile.

The men looked at her wearily. A couple of the men said something in Chinese. The man who had spoken to Mr. Ure, though, smiled a happy smile.

"I am the only one who speaks English," he said. "My name is Hop Sun. Can you free us? We are not comfortable this way."

Ty nodded, took out his pocket knife, and started cutting the rope. Minus sat to watch.

"Why did he tie you up?" Eva asked.

"If he had to dump us overboard, we'd all sink," said Hop Sun. "We wouldn't be able to swim, all tied together."

"Why would he have to dump you overboard?"

"The police suspect people are smuggling Chinese from Canada to America," Hop Sun said. "If the police spotted him, he could dump us overboard and not be caught."

Eva's eyes widened. "Oh my," she said. "You mean he would kill you!"

Hop Sun nodded, then smiled. "But he didn't. We are here, as you can see. It all worked out. And now, after you cut the rope, I will run into the woods here to hide."

"You will hide?" asked Eva in surprise.

He nodded. "All of us here were smuggled into this country at our own choosing. Unlike the other men who have just come from China, I have been in this country before. I worked for years laying railroad tracks across this great nation. Mr. Wong, a contractor from Tacoma, paid our way here from Canada. Tomorrow morning we will be sent to work in the mines of Wyoming. I want to stay here, though. I like the water. I don't want to work in the mines. That is why I will hide."

Hop Sun was very skinny. His dark quilted tunic hung baggily on his frame, its sleeves rolled up at the end to show his large hands, and long fingers. He had happy eyes and a wide smile. His ears stuck out a bit. His head was shaved except for the braid down his back. A skull cap sat on his head.

"We can help you," said Eva, her eyes shining. She liked adventures and drama, and Hop Sun's plan offered both.

After Ty cut the ropes, the men shuffled down to the water, wearily waiting for the boat that was to pick them up. Eva, Ty and Hop Sun walked over to where the woods began. Quietly they entered the woods. Minus followed them, and Ty squatted down, his arms around his dog to keep him from moving.

They hid there until they saw a little tugboat slowly make its way to the hidden dock. They watched a white man throw down a gangplank. He and a Chinese man wearing a western suit and bowler hat walked towards the bedraggled men.

The Chinese man appraised the men as if they were cattle.

"I thought that Ure was bringing 12 workers," said the Chinese man. "There are only 11 here. Is Ure trying to cheat me?"

Ty recognized the Chinese man as Mr. Wong who ran a grocery store in town. Mr. Wong and the white man talked in low voices for a bit, and then they herded the weary Chinese men on board. Mr. Wong gave every man a cup of water and a hard roll. Then the boat chugged off. When it was out of sight, Eva, Ty, and Hop Sun came back onto the beach. Minus had found a good smell in the middle of a rotting log.

"That was easy," Hop Sun said, with a big smile. "Now comes the hard part. Finding a place to stay and getting employment in Tacoma."

He looked at them happily. "But I've already made two friends in this city. Fortune has smiled on me, sending you two here. I will not be alone."

They started to walk back along the waterfront to the downtown. As they rounded the bend, they heard a voice say, "Stop right there."

They turned and saw the white man from Mr. Wong's boat standing in front of them. He smiled. "I think the Chinese fella there forgot where he was supposed to go. My boss, Mr. Wong, paid passage for twelve Chinamen to go on to the mines of Wyoming, and we got to send twelve."

He patted a gun tucked in a holster on his hip. "Come on buddy. We weren't born yesterday, ya know."

Ty and Eva looked at Hop Sun, alarmed. But he just smiled.

"Thank you," Hop Sun said to the man. "I had to relieve myself in the woods back there and was quite distressed to see you had left without me."

The white man laughed. "Glad to oblige you." Then he shot his gun in the air. "That's our signal for the boat to return to the private dock. Come on." He led Hop Sun back the way they came. Eva and Ty watched them until they disappeared around the bend. At the last second, Hop Sun turned and waved.

As Ty and Eva headed back home, they saw the little boat chugging past them, heading back to pick up Hop Sun.

"Isn't it funny how people can make an appearance in your life for just one day, and you'll never see them again?" asked Eva. "It is sheer chance that our paths crossed with Hop Sun. I wonder how he will like Wyoming?"

They walked along the waterfront, and a slight wind rustled up the water. The seagulls cried off in the distance. When they passed the Stanley Lumber Mill, they saw a long line of men, Chinese and white, waiting.

"What's going on?" Eva asked.

"Job openings," a man standing in line said. "We're hoping to get work."

A short man with a red face came out of the mill office. He wore a dark suit coat, dark pants and a white shirt with a high starched collar. Everyone in line quieted down.

"This company ain't employing any Chinese!" he shouted. "So Chinese, you can leave now!"

Eva looked puzzled. "Why?" she called out. "Chinese are good workers!"

"There ain't enough jobs for the white workers," the manager yelled back. "So here, whites get hired first."

"It's not fair," said Eva.

"It's not fair for them to always be working for less money," one white man in line grumbled. "Back at the other mill, when times got tough, the Chinese kept their jobs while we whites were let go."

The Chinese man standing next to him said quietly, "We got half the money white men got. We took the jobs because that's all that is offered us."

"I ain't saying no more!" the manager bellowed to everyone. "Chinese, go home. All of you." He went inside, and the Chinese men slowly stepped out of line.

"If I was Chinese, I'd protest vociferously," said Eva.

Maybe the Chinese had a lot more practice with bad treatment, Ty thought, because they didn't say anything. They just turned and walked away and the white men in line all stepped up, filling their places.

***

The next morning Ty and Minus visited Mrs. Low early. Ty had promised to take Eva fishing later in the afternoon but yet he still wanted to visit Mrs. Low (and get some food for Minus). Eva had never been fishing in her life, and Ty wanted to show her another joy of life in the great Northwest.

Mrs. Low was very interested to hear of their adventure with the smuggler and Hop Sun.

"A person's greed is like a snake that wants to swallow an elephant. Mr. Ure will get caught someday, and we will shoot off firecrackers to celebrate."

"I bet you would like Hop Sun," said Ty.

"I agree. He's clever," said Mrs. Low. "A smart rabbit running from the fox. Maybe someday we'll all go to Wyoming to meet him."

As Ty and Minus left the restaurant, Ty heard someone call out, "Hello!"

He looked up to see Hop Sun calmly walking across the street to Mr. Wong's Grocery Store.

"My old friend!" Hop Sun said, waving to Ty, a big smile on his face.

Just then, Mr. Wong ran out of his store. "What are you doing here?" he asked Hop Sun. "The wagon taking all of the men to Wyoming left early this morning. You should have been on it. You have cheated me!"

Hop Sun laughed as if they were all in on a funny joke. "Don't worry for a second," he said. "I found someone to take my place. I met another Chinese man who has been here a month without finding work. He wanted to go to Wyoming to work in the mines instead of me. So you have not been cheated. I will stay here. I like to be near water. It all works out. It is good."

Mr. Wong did not look happy. "You have tricked me. Don't expect me to help you here. You are on your own."

Again Hop Sun smiled. "I slept out under the stars last night. It will be good here. I will not need your help. Everything will work out."

Muttering, Mr. Wong turned around and went back into his store. Hop Sun turned to look at Ty.

"Hello again, my friend," he said. "This is indeed a coincidence."

Ty remembered how Eva had wondered how Hop Sun would get along in the future. Now they would be able to see for themselves.

CHAPTER 11: HOP SUN GETS A JOB
Opportunity is like catching the sun's rays.

As Ty stood on the street with Hop Sun, his stomach growled. He looked down at the food Mr. Low had given him and back up at Hop Sun.

"Hungry?" Ty asked, holding up the package.

Hop Sun's smile grew broader. "I was just saying to myself, what would make this day perfect? The view here is beautiful, I am in a wonderful new town. Last night I slept out under the stars. But, alas, I am hungry, and I have no money to buy food. And then – look! One of only two people I know here shows up with food. And he's willing to share. My grandmother often said, 'Divide an orange – it tastes just as good.' I am a lucky man indeed."

Ty, Minus, and Hop Sun walked down to the waterfront, found a log to sit on, and began eating what Mr. Low had wrapped up for them. Perhaps Mr. Low had a feeling Ty would need to share that day. He had included several beef bones with much meat still on them, as well as some heels of bread, some leftover cooked vegetables, and some rice that had been burned just a little. The cook's disappointment was joy to the hungry man, boy, and dog.

When every scrap of food was gone, Ty and Hop Sun sat back, satisfied. Minus ran off exploring.

"Now I will find work," said Hop Sun. "And I will find a place to live. Is there one area where the Chinese live?"

"Little Canton." said Ty, pointing down along the waterfront.

"Good," Hop Sun said. "Would you happen to know of any jobs?"

Ty wanted to laugh. He was an eleven-year-old boy, how would he know about jobs? But then a thought hit him. "My friend Mr. Low runs a restaurant."

"Would you introduce me?" Hop Sun asked. Ty nodded.

"Oh this is a wonderful life," said Hop Sun, sitting back and looking out at the sparkling waters of Puget Sound. "A friend who will share his food with me is a good friend, indeed. I will get to live by the water, which restores my soul. What could be better?" Hop Sun breathed in deeply, contentedly, surveying the scenery. "Ah, it is a life full of hope and possibilities."

Ty liked that. He was happy to see someone with such optimistic, buoyant spirit.

"Tomorrow when I pick up the leftovers, I will introduce you," Ty said.

Hop Sun rose, bowed, and headed down the waterfront to look for housing. Ty and Minus ran as fast as they could to Eva's house. She was going to be so excited to hear that Hop Sun was here.

***

The next afternoon, after Ty had played two games of chess with Mrs. Low – and had beaten her in one ("The student surpasses the teacher!" she said in mock dismay), he and Minus went to the back door of the restaurant. Hop Sun was already there, smiling. "My friend Ty and his dog, I greet you again." He bowed, and Ty bowed back.

"You will be pleased to know that I have found lodging," continued Hop Sun. "There is a bunk house in Little Canton where, for a small price, I may rent a bunk. That is all I need. A place to lay my head. A place to be sheltered when it rains."

Just then Mr. Low came out with his wrapped package of food scraps. He looked surprised to see Hop Sun standing with Ty.

"His name is Hop Sun," said Ty eagerly. "He wants to work. Can he work for you, Mr. Low?"

Mr. Low looked at Hop Sun. "Have you ever been a waiter, sir?" he asked. "Have you served food? My waiter left me a while ago."

Hop Sun smiled his joyous smile. "All my life, I've served food," he said. "Although I have never worked in a restaurant, I have cooked for my family and served them their food since I was young. And I am such a quick learner, especially when food is involved, that you will see I have many skills in this area."

"You are not modest," Mr. Low said.

"No," admitted Hop Sun. "Confidence and an eagerness to work hard will take me far."

First and foremost, Mr. Low was a business-man and he could see this young man before him had charm, a good quality in a restaurant worker.

"I like a worker like that," said Mr. Low. "I can pay very little, I'm sorry to say. Business is slow now because some people are boycotting us. However, you will get a little money and you will always eat." Hop Sun beamed.

And that was how Hop Sun got his job.

Unfortunately, Hop Sun's confidence and his ability were two different things.

"Who would think by looking at him, that he would always be dropping and spilling and stumbling over things?" asked Mr. Low. Hop Sun's clumsiness didn't seem to bother him in the least, and he charmed all of the customers he came in contact with. Mr. Low tried to teach him.

"Hop Sun, my friend," Mr. Low told him. "Take your time with the customers. We are in no rush. People come here to be relaxed in their dining and enjoy their food. You make them nervous!"

Hop Sun tried, but finally Mr. Low had to give him a new job in the kitchen where he helped chop, stir, and fry. There in the kitchen, he shone. There, he showed his true talent. He was an artist with his cooking (and the customers were safe from his eager clumsiness).

CHAPTER 12: RESCUING MINUS

A fallen tree will lean on its neighbor.

Ty was not used to getting noticed. Minus, however, received lots of attention. A dog with three legs fascinated people, and besides, Minus had such an open, friendly nature that folks were drawn to him. Ty always wondered where Minus had come from and what his history was. Then one day he found out.

A traveling peddler who sold and sharpened knives stopped Ty one day when he was walking down Pacific Avenue, on his way to Mr. Low's restaurant. Behind the peddler stood a shabby wagon hitched to a tired-looking old horse. A sign on the wagon read "Ichabod Stump's Pots, Pans, Knives and Knife Sharpening."

"Boy!"

Ty looked up. The peddler was addressing him.

"Boy, come over here."

Ty slowly went over to the peddler. Minus had lagged behind him to investigate some interesting garbage outside of the grocery store.

"That there is my dog," said the peddler. He was a small, wiry, scruffy-looking man, and he was pointing down the street at Minus. "I aim to take him back."

Ty's stomach tightened. He stared at the man, shocked.

The peddler spit and scratched his stubble of a beard. "I got that dog a year ago when it was a pup. A fella in Olympia couldn't pay for a knife, so I traded him. Then the dumb dog got his back leg caught in a bear trap. He was supposed to die. I left him behind and moved on. But look! That ornery cuss didn't die. Now I want him back. A three-legged dog like that would get me a lot of business. My next stop is Portland. Folks there will love him. He's rightfully mine."

Just then Minus came running up to Ty, wagging his tail. When he saw Ichabod Stump, he stopped and started backing away, growling.

Ichabod twisted his lips into a hard smile. "Come here, Mutt."

Minus turned and ran. Ty looked at the man, confused as to what he should do.

"Get me that dog, Boy," he said. "I aim to get that dog. It's mine, not yours."

Ty didn't know what to do. He'd never stood up to an adult before in his life. So he did the only thing he could think of. Like Minus, Ty took off running.

"Come back here, Boy," yelled the peddler. "That's my dog. I'll track you down. I'll find you."

Ty ran until he could run no more, and then he walked. He didn't know where Minus had gone, but he hoped the dog had enough sense to stay clear of the peddler. Ty headed to the woods, but Minus was nowhere to be seen. Minus loved most everyone, so the peddler must have been horrible to him. As Ty remembered what the peddler had told him, one thought struck him: how could a person just leave an injured dog to die? Who could do that?

For the whole next day Ty kept clear of downtown, not even going to get food from Mr. Low. But the next evening when Ty and Minus came back to the barn for the night, Pa was standing outside... with Ichabod Stump.

"That three-legged flea-bag belongs to this man," said Ty's pa. "Hand him over." Ty saw a new knife tucked into Pa's belt. Ichabod Stump must have given it to Pa in order to get the dog. For the first time in his life, Ty truly hated his pa. He traded his beloved dog for a cheap knife. Ty wouldn't trade him for a million dollars.

Ty shook his head. Pa swore, strode over, and whacked Ty in the head with his big calloused hand. "Give it to him," Pa said.

119

Tears ran down Ty's face, and his face ached from his pa's slap, but he shook his head again. Minus was hiding behind him, growling.

Ichabod Stump lunged at the dog and grabbed the scruff of his neck. "He's gonna make me a bundle," he said. "Everyone will know of me and my three-legged mutt."

Ty flung himself on the man, kicking and hitting him. His pa came over, grabbed him, and held his arms behind his back.

"Take that mutt and go," Pa ordered the man. "I can't hold this boy forever."

Ty was yelling now and kicking his pa, trying to get free. His pa shook him fiercely and then pushed him up against the side of the barn.

Ty's brothers ran up to see what was happening, and when they saw it was a fight, they cheered.

"Hit him again, Pa!" shouted Sam.

"Come on Ty," said Fred, laughing. "Kick him harder!"

Ichabod Stump put a rope around Minus' neck and dragged him off. Minus barked and tried to bite until the peddler tied another rope around his mouth to muzzle him. Then he threw the dog into the wagon, tied him to the front seat, and drove off.

When the wagon vanished from sight, Pa flung the still struggling Ty to the ground.

"Damn you," growled Pa and left. Ty laid on the ground, sobbing. His brothers, laughing, went into the house, leaving Ty all alone.

Ty couldn't stay there. He had to leave. Sore and sobbing, he opened the door to the barn to make sure Angel was in there. He threw some bread on the ground so the cat wouldn't starve, padlocked the barn so it'd be safe, and then he headed down to Eva's house.

When Mrs. Doyle opened the door, she was surprised to see Ty crying and shaking. Minus was nowhere to be seen.

"Ty, what happened?" she asked.

"Pa traded Minus for a knife," Ty said bitterly. He felt like his insides were bursting with hate.

"Did he hit you?" Mrs. Doyle asked, seeing the boy's bruised face. Ty just looked down. Mrs. Doyle swore under her breath. Eva looked at her mother in surprise. She'd never heard her mother swear before. Mrs. Doyle didn't care, she was angry.

"Well, first we'll get you cleaned up," she said. "You can stay here tonight. It's too late to do anything. Tomorrow we'll see if Chief Cooper will help us. The peddler's gone by now and it's late, but we'll get Minus back, if it's the last thing we do."

Eva got some soap and water, and Mrs. Doyle washed off the blood and dirt from Ty's face. Mrs. Doyle's anger had somehow calmed Ty. It meant she would do something. He'd never felt so determined about anything in his life. Minus would not live with that man. The goodness and joy of Minus couldn't exist under such an evil person. It just couldn't. Minus would surely die.

Early the next morning, Mrs. Doyle, Eva and Ty went to the police. Chief Cooper was in Seattle for the day. The assistant chief, Captain Maguire, was not any help.

"That Ichabod Stump is a mean one all right," said Captain Maguire. "But it sounds like it's his dog."

"But he abandoned it," said Mrs. Doyle, her voice rising. "Ty has taken care of it for weeks."

Captain Maguire shrugged. "It's just a dog. You can get another one, one with four legs."

Mrs. Doyle looked furious. "You sir, are a poor excuse for a police captain. And Chief Cooper will hear more about this later. We have a dog to rescue now." With that, she grabbed Ty's hand and Eva's hand and pulled them out of the door.

"Let's ask Mr. and Mrs. Low for help," said Eva. "Mrs. Low will no doubt have wisdom for this very occasion."

When Mr. and Mrs. Low heard the story, Mrs. Low looked at her husband fiercely. "That boy needs the dog. And the dog needs him," she said. "Go with them. I can manage here. To keep busy, I will plan a new menu and figure out how to arrange the tables for maximum efficiency. Go!"

Mr. Low looked at his wife with dismay. He knew better than to argue with her but now he had only Hop Sun and the cook to take care of the restaurant. He sighed.

"I better find that dog quickly before you have changed the whole restaurant," Mr. Low said. "Let us go now."

"He could have gone in any direction," said Mrs. Doyle. "North, South, East, West. How are we to know?

Ty thought for a second, trying to remember something that was in the back of his mind. Something the peddler had said. Ah! That was it. He said that people in Portland would love

Minus. "He said he was going south to Portland," said Ty.

"So if we follow him and find him, what do we do then?" asked Eva. "How do we take Minus from him?"

"We have to be smarter than he is," said Mrs. Doyle. "Look at us! If two heads are better than one, four heads are even better. Besides the peddler's head isn't very smart. We'll triumph."

***

Mr. Low rented a horse and wagon at the nearby livery stable, and he threw a satchel into the wagon, before climbing in.

"What is that?" asked Eva.

"I have a few items which may help us later," said Mr. Low. And off they went.

Ty didn't ever remember a time when he felt so nervous. His whole life depended on this. He had to get Minus back. He couldn't survive without his dog. Everything in his life was either "Before Minus" or "After Minus." After Minus included everything good: Eva and her mother, Hop Sun, Li, Minus, Angel and Mr. and Mrs. Low. Somehow Ty felt they were all connected. What if he couldn't get his dog back? He'd sink back into his old "Before Minus" life, the one that was dark, lonely, and hopeless. The thought made him shudder. "Faster," he whispered to no one in particular. "Faster."

The horse seemed to hear his words, because the old animal went as fast as he'd ever gone in his life. Ty kept thinking of what Eva had said, even if they found the peddler, how would they get Minus away from him?

Luck was with them. In the first town they came to, The Prairie, they saw a woman holding the hands of two little girls as they came out of a grocery store. "Have you seen a knife peddler?" Mrs. Doyle asked.

"A runty fellow? Smelly?" asked the woman. "Yes, indeed. I've already had my knives sharpened by him. Nasty little man but he knows his trade. Think he went over to the tavern for a drink."

"Was there a dog with him?" Eva asked eagerly.

The woman thought. "Girls, did he have a dog?" she asked her daughters. The girls giggled and shrugged.

Ty's heart started to pound. What if he had hurt Minus? But if he wanted to use the dog to attract customers, he wouldn't hurt him. But if Minus bit him ... Ty didn't want to think about it.

They walked down the main street of town, and there, outside one of the taverns, Ty spotted Ichabod Stump's wagon. He ran over to see if Minus was in it. The cluttered wagon was filled with knives, clothes, pots, and pans, but no dog.

"Maybe that horrid man brought Minus into the tavern," said Mrs. Doyle. "There's one way to find out. Come on." Eva and Ty looked at each other. Were children even allowed in a tavern?

Mr. Low, his face serious, carried his satchel through the tavern doors, followed by Mrs. Doyle, Eva and Ty. The lighting inside was dim. Right away, Ty spotted Ichabod Stump sitting at the bar, and there – tied to a chair with the rope muzzle still on him was Minus, looking downright miserable.

Ty ran over to Minus and threw himself on his dog. Minus was tied so tightly with a short leash, he couldn't move. The muzzle kept him from barking, but he squealed in joy and squirmed madly.

Ichabod Stump, who had already had three or four drinks, recognized the boy, pushed his chair back and stood up. "You followed me?" he asked drunkenly. "Who did you bring?"

The peddler looked at the odd group: the shabby little boy, a redheaded girl, a slim woman with steely eyes, and a middle-aged, frowning, Chinese man. He snorted.

Mrs. Doyle spoke first. "You took this boy's dog, Mr. Ichabod Stump. We're taking him back."

Ichabod Stump gave Minus a nudge with his dirty boot. "This here dog is mine. I got him last year. He didn't die, so he's still mine."

Mr. Low stepped forward and said, "Please untie the dog and return him to the boy."

Ty hugged Minus so tightly he could feel the dog's heart beating fast.

Then Ichabod took out his sharp knife. The other men at the bar looked alarmed and stood up, slowly backing away. Ichabod smirked at Mr. Low.

"Want me to cut off that pigtail, sissy?" he asked Mr. Low. He was showing off.

Mr. Low's face did not change. "No, I do not wish that," he said.

"I'll cut a lot more if you all don't clear out of here," Ichabod said, weaving a bit.

Then Ty saw that Mr. Low opened the satchel and took something out: his own knife. Ty's eyes widened. Would they have a knife fight? He didn't want Mr. Low to get hurt.

Mr. Low handed the knife to Ty. "Cut the rope," he said. "Free the dog."

Ichabod turned to Ty and pointed the knife. "Don't touch that rope, boy."

Ty only wanted his dog to be free; he didn't care one whit what happened to himself. He started cutting the rope. Mr. Low's knife was so sharp that it wouldn't take long

"What did I say, boy?" growled Ichabod and lunged for Ty, knife out.

In one second, Mr. Low blocked Ichabod's arm, and with his other hand, grabbed the man's elbow, twisting his wrist, pulling his arm up, and pushing him down to the ground.

"Why you..." said Ichabod, scrambling back up to his feet. He forgot about Ty now and was concentrating solely on Mr. Low. Ichabod blinked as if to clear his eyes and then lunged at Mr. Low, his knife in hand, and once again Mr. Low blocked, grabbed, twisted, and tripped the peddler, sending him sprawling on the floor.

This time Ichabod's knife clattered to the floor. Mrs. Doyle quickly ran over and picked it up.

Now Ichabod didn't look so brave. He'd lost his knife, he still was woozy from the alcohol, and he realized he was in the presence of a man who knew how to fight.

By this time, Ty had freed Minus and had yanked the muzzle off. Minus barked and ran around in circles.

Mr. Low looked at the pathetic peddler. "We will be leaving now. <u>With</u> the dog. Please do not return to Tacoma in the future. Thank you."

Ichabod got to his knees and wiped his nose. He had lost, and he knew it. He shrugged and muttered "That stupid mutt was more trouble than he was worth. Good riddance."

Eva, Mrs. Doyle, Mr. Low and Ty, with Minus firmly in his master's arms, went to the wagon. Mrs. Doyle was still holding the peddler's sharp knife.

"What are you going to do with that?" Eva asked.

"I know he has more where this came from, but still, I don't want this knife to ever hurt a living creature," said Mrs. Doyle. She walked over to a nearby rose bush and using the knife blade as a shovel, dug a hole in the dirt. Then she buried the knife and stamped dirt on top. They all got into the wagon and headed back to Tacoma.

"How did you learn to fight like that?" Eva asked Mr. Low, as they rode.

"When I was young I studied an ancient Chinese defense," said Mr. Low. "I am not a violent person, but there are times when defense is handy. To tell the truth I was nervous that I had forgotten what to do."

"You were very impressive," said Mrs. Doyle. "Ichabod Stump didn't know with whom he was dealing."

"Mrs. Low will be happy," said Mr. Low, looking over at Ty. The small boy was bent over Minus, his face in his fur, hugging him tightly. "I hope she has not done too much damage to the restaurant."

Ty had his dog. There was nothing more that he wanted. Never had a dog been so tightly hugged. Ty would never let him go. Ever.

Halfway home, he lifted his face from his dog. He looked at Mr. Low who was holding the reins to the horse and listening to Mrs. Doyle, at Eva who was smiling at Minus. Ty suddenly realized that he'd never had anyone stand up for him before. Mr. Low, Mrs. Doyle, and Eva were true friends. That feeling so overwhelmed the boy that he buried his face in his dog's fur again, so no one could see his tears.

CHAPTER 13: FOURTH OF JULY

Every day cannot be a feast of lanterns.

Ty was afraid that his pa would make him return the dog to the peddler, but it turned out that his pa didn't care.

"I got a knife out of it, so the peddler was the loser, not me. Just keep that dog away from me," he told Ty. Ty made every effort to do so.

Summer proceeded at a leisurely pace. Every morning Ty worked with Mrs. Doyle on his reading. She'd give him some breakfast and, for as much time as she could spare, attempted to teach him. He still didn't understand why reading was so hard for him. Using the typewriter to learn words seemed to help. Progress was slow, but bit by bit, he was learning. After the lesson, Eva read to him and Li from one of her books, and then they went outside to explore.

In the afternoon, Ty and Minus would go by the restaurant to visit Mrs. Low, do some errands for Mr. Low, and eat. A comforting routine.

The Fourth of July was fast approaching. Ty had lived in Tacoma for several years and knew the city had a celebration to be proud of. Every year he'd go down to Pacific Avenue to watch the parade. Seeing the bands march, the Puyallup Tribe of Indians ride their gallant horses, and the decorated wagons roll down the street thrilled Ty.

This year Eva wanted to go with him. "I adore parades," she said. "In New York, there's a parade for every occasion. Next year if I'm back there I can tell my friends about this patriotic parade from out west. I'm sure it'll be marvelous."

Ty didn't like that she was talking about going back to New York. Eva was his first friend ever, and he didn't know what he'd do without her. Besides, what if it took Mrs. Doyle longer than a year to teach him to read? He would never learn then.

Ty was practical, though. Eva was here now, so he wasn't going to worry much about next year. Plenty of time to worry later.

The parade started at ten o'clock in the morning. Ty and Minus were at Eva's house by nine, hoping, perhaps, they'd get some food. Their faith was rewarded. Mrs. Doyle gave Ty some fried eggs and biscuits. Minus got a couple of biscuits too. Then Eva, Ty, and Minus walked to Pacific Avenue.

People were already lining the street. Occasionally someone would notice Minus and yell out, "That dog has only three legs!" as if Ty didn't know.

As they maneuvered to get to the front of the crowd, Mr. Sundstrom, a jovial fellow who owned the candy shop, yelled out to them, "That three-legged dog should be in the parade."

Ty secretly agreed. Minus should be properly honored, maybe with his own float. That thought made Ty smile. Eva, though, took Mr. Sundstrom's bait and yelled back, "What will you give us, if he does?"

Mr. Sundstrom laughed. "A free bag of candy for the both of you," he shouted.

Eva looked at Ty. "Want to do it?" she asked. Ty thought for a second. He'd hardly ever had candy. Maybe once at school someone brought some homemade taffy to share with the class, but he'd never had anything store bought. And never a whole bag. He didn't like being the center of attention – but a whole bag of candy! It'd be worth it. "All right," he said.

Eva shouted back to Mr. Sundstrom, "It's a deal!" She took the scarf from around her head and tied it around Minus' neck, giving him a jaunty air. The scruffy dog seemed quite pleased with his new look.

"Ty, play your harmonica," Eva suggested. "You'll be our own marching band."

Ty had never performed in public before, but he did think Minus needed some musical accompaniment. So he took out his harmonica and began playing all the tunes he knew well beginning with: "Way Down Upon the Swanee River," "Row, Row, Row Your Boat," and "Sweet Betsy From Pike."

The three of them marched right behind the float with high school girls dressed to represent the 38 states of the United States and ahead of the fire department with its two wagons.

Minus was the hit of the parade. People were used to seeing marching bands, horses, and floats. But when they saw a raggedy boy playing a harmonica, a girl with flaming red hair and a three-legged dog wearing a green kerchief, the crowd cheered. Ty felt so proud that his chest almost hurt.

Near the end of the parade, though, Minus stopped in his tracks and his nose started quivering, as if he smelled something.

"Keep going, Minus," said Eva. "Or the fire wagons will run us down." Suddenly Minus broke rank and ran to a building. He started barking furiously. People nearby laughed at him.

Ty and Eva ran over to pull him back into the parade, when Ty noticed something.

"Look," he said. Eva looked and saw smoke coming out of the building.

"Fire," she yelled. "Fire, fire, fire!"

The fire department had been right behind them in the parade, so the firemen soon took control. People shouted, Minus barked, and the brass bands, not knowing what was happening, kept playing.

"Tacoma sure has a lot of fires," Eva said as they watched the firemen work.

A woman standing next to them had a grim expression on her face. "That one was set on purpose," she said.

Eva looked at her in surprise. "Why?" she asked.

"That shop is run by Bing Chong," the woman said. "Some folks want him to leave town because he's Chinese. I'm sure someone just now decided to 'encourage' him to get out."

Bing Chong himself was pacing up and down the sidewalk, distraught. "I leave today," he said. "They have gone too far. I am afraid for my life."

Eva and Ty rejoined the parade with Minus feeling unsettled. What if someone tried to burn down Mr. and Mrs. Low's restaurant? People had already broken the glass in their front window – more than once.

After the parade ended, Eva and Ty took their prize-winning dog back to the candy store. Mr. Sundstrom was in a good mood because business had been excellent that day.

"That is one special dog," Mr. Sundstrom said, filling up a small bag of candies. He handed it to Eva, and then started filling up one for Ty. He scooped in butterscotch pieces, peppermints and caramels.

Outside the shop, Minus whined. He wanted treats too.

"Is candy good for dogs?" Ty asked Mr. Sundstrom.

The merchant laughed. "Probably not, but look, here's a broken cookie. He can eat that." He handed Ty two halves of a big cookie.

Ty fed the cookie pieces to the eager dog who turned around in circles to try to get more. Ty laughed at his happy, clever dog.

He unwrapped a butterscotch piece and sucked it. The warm sweetness filled his mouth. This was heaven, Ty thought. Candy, a parade, and being with Eva and Minus. It would have been a perfect day – except for the fire.

***

That evening Mrs. Doyle made a picnic to take to the downtown park. There people gathered to hear the town band play patriotic music and to socialize. Hop Sun and Li were also invited to share Mrs. Doyle's basket of goodies and to experience a real American holiday. Ty watched as Hop Sun tried to walk next to Li. She was polite but maneuvered away from him. Ty was puzzled. Why wouldn't Li like Hop Sun? He was the happiest, nicest man Ty had ever met.

Mrs. Doyle spread a quilt on the ground, and from the basket she took fried chicken, potato salad, biscuits, and a big chocolate cake for dessert. Dusk was settling in now, and soon the sky would be dark enough for fireworks. The picnickers finished their food and were enjoying the music when Mayor Weisbach and a few of his friend strolled by.

The mayor recognized Mrs. Doyle and strode over to the little group's picnic.

"So this is the young woman who ran away," Mayor Weisbach said in a jolly, loud voice, nodding his head at Li. "Enjoying fine American food on a fine American holiday, are you?"

Mrs. Doyle sat up straighter on her blanket. "We are all enjoying this holiday," she said.

"Good," said the mayor, smiling. "This may be the last holiday you'll be able to celebrate with the Chinese." His friends laughed and nodded in agreement.

Mrs. Doyle shook her head. "If the Chinese leave, it would be bad luck for Tacoma," she said. "They contribute to our town. Besides, The Declaration of Independence says all men are created equal. Are you saying you don't believe in that?"

"Equal, ja! In their own country," said the mayor, slightly irritated. "Good day, ma'am." And he turned and walked off with his friends running to keep up to him.

When Ty watched the scene between Mrs. Doyle and the mayor, he started to get that familiar bad feeling in the pit of his stomach.

After the mayor left, a drunken man who had overheard their conversation belligerently swaggered up to them. He reached down, grabbed

Hop Sun by his tunic, and dragged him off the blanket. "Chinaman, go home!" he slurred.

A middle-aged farmer came over to help Hop Sun, and the drunken man pushed him away. "Don't defend 'em," he said. "Chinamen shouldn't be eating with our women and children."

People around them started to get involved in the argument, yelling and pushing. Hop Sun and Li stood up, ready to leave, if they had to. Just then, the worst thing happened: Ty's pa came out of the tavern and heard the commotion. He took one look at Ty standing with Hop Sun and Li, and he roared over to them. Pa grabbed Ty by the collar of his shirt and hoisted him up off his feet. Ty could smell beer.

Pa's eyes were wild. "Get home now," he yelled, "And if I ever catch you with Chinese vermin again, I'll break both of your legs and kill that dog."

Ty knew Pa was capable of doing anything when he was drunk. He ran with Minus following him. He could hear his pa yelling and swearing still, as he ran.

He could also hear Eva yelling, "Ty! Come back!"

Suddenly he heard a sharp crack and some pops. Was Pa shooting at him now? But no, the sky flickered with light. Ty turned and saw that the black sky over the waterfront was filled with colors. The fireworks had begun.

CHAPTER 14: HOP SUN IS ACCUSED

An optimist sees an opportunity in every calamity;
a pessimist sees a calamity.

Back in his bed in the barn, with his dog to his side and his cat at his feet, Ty tried to figure out if Pa meant what he said. He was drunk when he said it, and often he forgot what he said or did when he was that way. Ty looked up at the moonlight coming through the slats of the barn ceiling. Should he risk Pa's anger?

If he gave up his friends, he would return to how he was, how he used to live. More than anything, his friends gave him hope...hope that he could learn to read, hope that he'd grow up someday and maybe even see New York City, hope that he could get away from his pa.

The answer was clear. He had to see his friends. He'd try to stay out of his pa's way, but Mr. and Mrs. Low needed him. Li and Hop Sun made him happy. Eva and Mrs. Doyle were changing his life.

He surely hoped Pa had been so drunk he wouldn't remember anything. He surely hoped that.

***

Hop Sun was a happy man, optimistic by nature. "Everything will work out," he said frequently. "Despite life's ups and downs, in the end, all will be well. Wherever I end up, I will find happiness."

Unfortunately, Mr. Low's restaurant was struggling. "Mayor Weisbach has been leading a boycott on all Chinese establishments," said Mr. Low. "It has taken its toll on my business. Hop Sun, I'm afraid I can no longer afford to hire you here. I can keep only the old cook. I will be the only waiter. I am very sorry."

Hop Sun nodded and smiled. "I understand," he said. "It will all work out."

Mr. Low shook his head. He was a businessman, an ambitious one at that. He didn't want to just "get by." He wanted to make money. He had plans! He wanted to buy land and buildings, and perhaps start another restaurant. Hop Sun was a nice young man, but too naïve, thinking everything would always work out. Mr. Low knew very well that sometimes things didn't work out.

Later that day, however, Mr. Low heard that Ah Wing's laundry worker couldn't stand the pressure of Mayor Weisbach's group and had left for California that day. Mr. Wing needed a new employee, and when Hop Sun asked for the job, he was hired immediately. Perhaps, Mr. Low thought, Hop Sun was born lucky.

Laundry work meant Hop Sun had to stand over steaming, boiling vats of water, stirring the clothes with a stick. After the clothes were washed and dried, he pressed them with a hot heavy iron. The work started early and ended late, with only one day off a week. The pay was low. One benefit, though, was Hop Sun could live in a back room, saving money on rent.

Ah Wing was worried that his business would not be able to survive Mayor Weisbach's boycotts. "They'll starve us out of here," he told Hop Sun. "How will we survive?"

Hop Sun just smiled. "We work very hard," he said. "That is an ingredient for success."

Ah Wing still looked worried. "I could move to Portland," he said. "Or San Francisco. But that means I have to start all over."

"It will all work out," said Hop Sun, and he seemed so sure of himself, Ah Wing almost believed him.

***

One morning in late July Hop Sun's optimism and confidence was tested. Ah Wing and Hop Sun had already been working for several hours when a young policeman came into the laundry.

"Please come with me," the policeman said to Hop Sun. "Miss Susan Matthews has accused you of assaulting her last night."

Hop Sun looked confused. Ah Wing came out from the back. "What is happening?" he asked.

"Your worker here attacked a young white woman last night," the policeman said. "She was coming home from work as a barmaid at McCormick's Tavern. This man jumped out from behind some bushes and stole her purse, beating her and pushing her to the ground. Her face is bruised and she has abrasions on her arms and legs."

"I do not know what you are talking about," said Hop Sun, puzzled.

"That's what they all say," the policeman said, escorting Hop Sun out of the laundry. "Off to jail for you."

***

Ty was in the middle of a reading lesson that morning and for the first time ever, he was reading a book. True, the book was for six-year-olds, but still, he knew every word. Then a distraught Ah Wing burst into the house and told them the news about Hop Sun.

144

"It's her word against his," said Eva, furious. "Why do police always believe someone who can cry crocodile tears? Why do they believe a white person over a Chinese person?"

Ah Wing shook his head. "I do not know," he said. "How could Hop Sun have done this?"

"Mrs. Matthews is not telling the truth," said Mrs. Doyle. "Did Mayor Weisbach pay her to lie? Did someone else from the anti-Chinese group tell her to do this to dishonor the Chinese? I smell a rat."

Ty, startled, looked around for a rodent running by, but then realized Mrs. Doyle was just using a saying.

"How can we prove that?" asked Eva. She looked at Ty. "Do you have any ideas, Ty?"

Ty frowned and tried to think. How could they prove that Hop Sun was innocent? His mind started working.

"Well, first we need to talk to Hop Sun," he said. After that, he had no ideas.

"You two will have to take care of this for now," said Mrs. Doyle. "I can't afford to miss my deadline. I'll help as soon as this stack of letters is done."

Ty and Eva walked over to the jailhouse which was located next to the police station.

145

"May we see Hop Sun?" Eva asked the jailer

"I don't know if he's allowed visitors," grumbled the jailer.

"He is," said Eva with such assurance that the jailer shrugged and led them to Hop Sun's cell.

"My friends!" exclaimed Hop Sun joyously. "I knew someone would come."

"Hop Sun, where were you last night? What happened? Did you know this woman?" asked Eva.

Hop Sun shook his head helplessly. "Last night, from the laundry I went to work at the Barrel Factory. I worked there two hours and when I got off, I went to the waterfront to pick up seaweed for cooking. It's the only time I have to do so," he said. "I love walking by the water, seeing the boats, smelling the sea air. As I came back to the downtown area, I saw a young woman, walking down the street, sobbing. Her lip was bleeding, her eye was swollen. I asked her if she needed help. She said she'd fallen, but I didn't believe her. You can't get those injuries from falling. I helped her to her home. Then I bid her a good evening, and returned to my room behind the laundry."

"She repaid your kindness by accusing you of hurting her," said Eva.

"Why would she do that?" asked Hop Sun. "We are taught never to repay kindness with evil or honesty with lies."

Eva looked at Ty. "Now what?" she asked. Ty thought for a second. Why would Eva think he'd know what to do? Did he have any insights?

"I guess now we need to talk to the woman," said Ty. "We have to find the truth."

Eva's eyes started to shine. "The truth! Mrs. Low says 'A mud figure fears rain; a lie fears truth,'" she said. "We'll start by finding out where Susan Matthews lives."

They said good-bye to Hop Sun and went past the jailer to the Police Station next door. There, at the counter, an older man, a clerk with a bushy white moustache, was filling out papers.

"Sir, my mother is a friend of Susan Matthews, the woman who was hurt last night," said Eva. "Mother went to visit her and locked us out of the house. My brother and I need to find her." Tears came to Eva's eyes. "Will you be so kind as to tell me where Susan lives? I think on 11th Street?"

She looked up at the jailer with imploring eyes.

The clerk felt sorry for the sweet little girl. He shuffled through the papers on his desk. "No honey, Miss Matthews lives on 9th and Railroad."

Eva looked concerned. "I don't remember what she looks like. My mother has bunches of friends. Is she a woman of about thirty, with long blonde hair?"

"Not at all," said the clerk kindly. The little red-headed girl seemed so simple and sweet that he was glad to help her. "Susan Matthews is in her twenties, with frizzy black hair and a few extra pounds on her. She looks a bit hard, if you know what I mean, but then, when I saw her she had just been assaulted by some no-good Chinaman."

"Thank you so much," said Eva with a sigh. "I hope I find my mother."

Ty, Eva and Minus walked over to 9th and Railroad, a neighborhood of cheap little houses. How could they find Miss Matthews?

"We can start knocking," said Ty. He was glad Eva was so friendly that she wouldn't mind knocking on strangers' doors. He'd hate it.

An elderly woman opened the first door Eva knocked on. "I'm looking for Susan Matthews," said Eva.

"Why?" the elderly woman asked suspiciously. "Is that tramp in trouble again?"

"No, she's a friend of my mother," said Eva. The woman pursed her lips, as if any friend of Susan's was not a nice person.

"She and her man live in that red house on the corner. Be careful though. That man is mean."

"Thank you," Eva said. The woman closed the door and Eva turned to Ty. "Let's meet Susan Matthews."

Ty wondered what sort of trouble they could be walking into, but they headed to the shabby little red house. Eva knocked on the door.

A young woman, plump and frizzy-haired, answered the door. Obviously this was Susan Matthews because she had a black eye, cuts on her face and scrapes on her arms.

"Yes?" she said, opening the door just a crack.

"Hello," said Eva. "My friend Ty and I are looking for Susan Matthews. We have a letter for her." Ty looked at Eva in astonishment. They had no letter.

"A letter!" said the woman. "Who would be writing me?"

"Are you Susan Matthews?" asked Eva.

"Yes," said the woman nervously, opening the door wider.

"I believe it's from a judge," said Eva. "The clerk who gave it to me said they caught you lying to them about the Chinese man you claimed assaulted you."

The woman's eyes grew large with fright. She took a step back. "It wasn't my idea," she whispered. "He made me do it."

"Who?" asked Eva innocently.

"Elmer. We was arguing. I made liver for dinner, and he don't like liver, and he beat me up something bad. How was I to know he don't like liver? I ran out of the house but I didn't have nowhere else to go, so I had to come back after a bit. When Elmer seen my face all puffed up and sore, he knew he could get in trouble 'cause he's done that before. He said I had to tell the police that a Chinese man did it. Elmer wants them Chinese out of Tacoma. I'd seen that tall skinny Chinaman carrying a bucket of seaweed when I went outside, so I thought...."

"I can't find that letter now, oh dear," said Eva, pretending to look. "I must have left it. Well, you come with me. My uncle is a lawyer, and I bet he'll help you. You probably won't have to go to jail for false testimony."

"I could go to jail?" Susan asked, alarmed. "But it weren't my fault, I tell you. Elmer beats me something awful if I don't do what he says."

"Then they'll understand for sure," said Eva. "Come with me now, before the charges are actually filed. Once they're filed, the police can't do anything about it. Is Elmer home now?" Eva smiled a sweet, concerned smile at the distraught woman.

"Not yet," Susan said, looking down the street. "Could be anytime."

"Let's hurry then," said Eva. "Tell the police. They're so nice."

The woman started crying, and Eva sympathetically took her by the arm and led her out the door. The three of them walked to the police station.

The policeman sitting at the front desk looked up at them, surprised to see the sweet redheaded girl back so soon.

"This is Miss Susan Matthews," said Eva. "She has something to say."

Susan Matthews burst into tears. "It wasn't my fault. He made me lie. Elmer hit me, not the Chinaman. But he made me tell the police that story. Don't arrest me. Please. I don't want to go to jail."

Tears streamed down her face, and her nose was running. "I don't know how you found out I lied, but it weren't my fault," she blubbered.

The police officer looked surprised. "You lied?" he asked. "This is news."

The woman looked alarmed. Then she looked at Eva. "But you said they had a warrant for my arrest."

Eva looked innocent, with wide eyes. "Oh dear. I might have gotten confused," she said. "Hop Sun, the man you accused, is a friend of ours, and I was pretty upset he was accused unjustly."

Susan started moaning. "Elmer will kill me, for sure," she said.

The police officer narrowed his eyes. "No he won't, ma'am," he said. "We'll make sure of that. It may not be illegal for him to hit you, but we sure don't like men who beat up their wives. We can make life mighty unpleasant for him. He won't want to do that again."

The policeman told the jailer to release Hop Sun.

When Hop Sun was a free man once more, he grinned happily at them. "See," he said. "It all works out. I got a day off work. A vacation! They had good food in jail too."

"And maybe we helped Susan from getting hurt by her mean husband," said Eva. "Not a bad day's work."

Ty bent down to scratch Minus. He was so relieved that Hop Sun was coming home.

CHAPTER 15: BOMB!
Wind isn't always favorable;
soldiers aren't always victorious.

Late one afternoon when Ty was picking up spices for Mr. Low at Meier's Grocery Store, he overheard three men in the store talking.

"Hewitt's not going along."

"Hewitt?"

"The Barrel Factory on the waterfront."

"He's not going along?"

"He won't fire his Chinese workers."

"...setting a bad example."

"That's right."

"...got to talk to him."

"Now?"

"Good a time as any."

And then they dropped their voices. Ty watched them leave the store.

Hewitt's Barrel Factory was where Hop Sun worked for an hour or two at the end of the day, sweeping, washing floors, discarding the end pieces of metal and wood, and taking out the garbage.

Ty was not an impulsive boy, but he just didn't like the tone and topic of the men's conversation. That bad feeling started churning his insides. The spices could wait. He needed to find out what they were up to. He'd follow them down to the waterfront to see if he could learn anything. The men strolled down the street, talking as they went. Ty and Minus kept a half-block behind them.

When the men reached the barrel factory, Ty went up the hill across the road where he could watch. He saw the men knock on the door of the building that said Office. (Ty was proud he could read that word.) Mr. Hewitt opened the door.

From his vantage point, Ty could see the three men talking while Mr. Hewitt shook his head. He didn't invite the men into his office. Ty couldn't hear what the men were saying but he could hear the rising pitch of their voices. Mr. Hewitt's voice got louder too. He tried to close the door but one of the men pushed it back open with his body.

Then Ty saw Mr. Hewitt pull out a large revolver from his coat. The three men started backing away.

"I'll hire who I want! Now GO!" shouted Mr. Hewitt, waving the revolver. Then he slammed the door.

Ty could tell, even from afar, that the three men weren't happy. He waited till the men were past him, and then he and Minus followed. He could hear the men's voices.

"...oh he'll be sorry, all right," one told the others. "If he gets away with it, others will think they can. ...get it and come back..." And then Ty couldn't hear anymore.

Who could he talk to about what he'd heard? Eva and her mother had gone to Seattle for an outing. Mr. Low would be busy at the restaurant now. That left Li. Would she be able to help him? He and Minus ran to Eva's house and knocked on the door.

Li was surprised to see him.

"We must go down there right now," Li said, when Ty explained. "Hop Sun may be in trouble."

Ty nodded, and the three of them set off.

Down at the factory, all was quiet. Mr. Hewitt and the factory workers had gone home for the day. The factory was built over the water, so logs could be easily floated there. Minus ran down the dock, looked around, decided the beach was more fun and ran back down the dock to chase seagulls on the shore.

"Where is Hop Sun?" Li asked. They walked a little further into the courtyard where barrels and parts of barrels were scattered around. There was no sign of their friend.

They had walked past a stack of barrel slats when they heard men's voices. Li quickly pulled Ty down behind a barrel. They peered out through a gap in the slats.

Two men walked briskly down the dock and into the courtyard. The younger of the two men was holding a burlap sack very gingerly.

"This makes me nervous," he muttered. "I hate holding this thing."

"You're a baby," said the older man. "We're here now. Just put it down where McKnight told us to, and then let's get the hell out of here."

"I ain't no baby," grumbled the younger man. "This could go off."

"You got to light it first," said the older man. "And then you got a couple of minutes before it explodes."

"You light it. I ain't getting near it."

"Baby."

"I ain't no baby!"

And then they went around the building, out of sight.

Ty looked at Li. She put her finger to her lip. "Shhh. They will come back."

Just then – to Ty's horror – Minus came running up the dock. The dog would give them away!

Minus reached the courtyard just as the men returned without the bag.

"Hey, what's that dog doing here? He's gonna be blown up!" said the younger man.

"Leave it. It's just a dog. A three-legged dog, at that." And the older man started running.

The younger man grabbed Minus by the scruff of his neck and pulled him towards land. Minus wriggled out of his grasp.

"Fool," said the younger man. "I was just trying to help you." And he too, started running.

The second that the men were out of sight, Ty and Li jumped up. "Hop Sun!" Li yelled. There was no answer. Then Li shouted out some words in Chinese.

At that moment Hop Sun appeared around the corner carrying a broom and dust pan. When he recognized his friends he smiled broadly.

"Hello!" he said, waving.

Li yelled something in Chinese.

Hop Sun looked surprised, then alarmed, and then he started towards them. He got halfway when – BOOM! Hop Sun was thrown in the air. Smoke covered everything. Ty desperately tried to see where Hop Sun landed. Bits of wood and paper floated down to the ground.

There! There he was...on the ground, crumpled, motionless. One of his shoes had been blown off, his clothes were torn, blood was everywhere. His face was covered with ash. Was he alive or dead? They ran to him.

Li knelt and spoke to him softly, urgently, in Chinese. Time froze. Was he alive? Terror filled Ty. What if his friend was dead?

Then Minus ran up and started barking. Hop Sun moaned. Never had a moan sounded so good.

Hop Sun moaned again and moved. He struggled to open his eyes. Li spoke to him in Chinese, and he said a couple words back to her. What were they saying, Ty wondered.

While Hop Sun struggled to sit up, Li wound her kerchief around his leg to stop the blood. Hop Sun winced with pain, looked at Ty, and a very weak but typical Hop Sun smile crossed his face. "Hello Ty," he whispered. "Nice to see you."

"Look," said Li, pointing toward the factory.

Ty and Hop Sun both turned. A chunk of the barrel factory was gone. Bits of the building floated in the water below.

Li and Ty helped Hop Sun to his feet. He staggered and crumpled again. "I do not seem to have the strength to walk," he said. And then he fainted.

Just then people started running up to the dock. They'd heard the explosion and seen the smoke.

Ty saw off in the distance that horses pulling a fire department wagon were racing towards them. "Good," said Li. "They can help Hop Sun get home."

Since there was no fire to put out, the firemen carefully put Hop Sun into the wagon so they could take him to a doctor. Ty and Li started their walk home, with Minus happily trotting beside them. Minus had no idea that Hop Son had been badly injured. All was well in the dog's life. He had chased countless birds and sniffed many logs that day. Ty wished he could be as happy and as carefree as his dog.

"If we had not gone down there, Hop Sun would have died," said Li in a hushed voice. "He would have been in that part of the factory that exploded."

Ty didn't say anything; he didn't want to think about that possibility. They continued to walk in silence.

"It was fate," Li said at last. "Fate."

The next day they read about the bombing in the newspaper. Mr. Hewitt was quoted as saying, "I give up. When I rebuild my factory, I will not be hiring any Chinese. I can't afford it."

The anti-Chinese had won that round.

***

Hop Sun needed a few weeks to recover from his injuries. He stayed in his room in the back of the laundry to recuperate, and every day Li brought him food. As he got a little stronger, the two of them would walk back down to Little Canton where his old bunkhouse was. Sometimes Eva, Ty and Minus joined them.

The Chinese bunkhouse was built by the waterfront, on one side of the railroad tracks. On the other side of the tracks was a big garden where the Chinese men grew vegetables. Ducks, pigs, and chickens roamed around the area. Minus loved chasing the chickens. He seemed to be laughing as he made them flap their wings, squawk and run.

Ty was curious about one thing. Why did the bunkhouse have so many beds jammed into one room? Why did so many men cram into such a small space?

"All of the men in the bunkhouse have one goal," Hop Sun told Ty. "We want to send as much money as we can to our families back in China. We all would like to sleep in a soft bed in a spacious home. We all would like to relax once in a while. But in our mind's eye, we see the faces of our mothers, our sisters, our fathers, our uncles…and they are starving. So we share one room, and we work hard and send home all our money."

***

As Hop Sun recuperated, he told them stories of his life.

"Conditions in China – bad," Hop Sun said. "My family starving. What could I do? I was a strong young man, willing to work, but there were no jobs, no money, no food. Then one day I see men on the streets hand out flyers. Flyers say, 'Come to America. Strong men are needed to build railroad. In America poor and rich men are equal. Much money is to be made in America.' And so I sign up to come. I get to this land and find work building the railroad. It is hard work. The white men get paid more than we do. We are given the worst jobs to do, the most dangerous. But at least we are paid."

"One time, when we used dynamite to blast a rock cave, twenty charges were placed and ignited, but only eighteen blasts went off. Our foreman thought two were duds. He ordered the Chinese workers to go into the cave. As they entered, the remaining charges exploded. Bodies flew from the cave as if shot from a cannon. Six of my friends were killed."

Ty looked at Hop Sun in shock. He'd seen men killed, his friends blown up. Who buried the dead men, Ty wondered. Who wrote their families? What happened to the families? They not only lost loved ones, they also lost their source of money.

On another day, Ty, Eva, and Li found out how Hop Sun made his way to Canada.

"When the train track across America was finished, we were all on the west coast," said Hop Sun. "Many Chinese were trying to find work. I wanted to see if Canada had more jobs. For a time, I was able to work, but then no jobs. I heard about Mr. Ure's ship coming back to this area. I got on it, and here I am. Who would think that I escaped the dynamite used to blast mountains only to be hurt by dynamite used to blast Chinese."

"Do you want to go back to China?" Eva asked.

Hop Sun looked thoughtful. "Most of the men want to go back when they've struck it rich. But not me. I want to stay here. There is opportunity here. I was a poor laborer in China and had no hopes of becoming anything more than a poor laborer. It is a hard life. But I like to work. I like people. I can have a better life here."

Then he held up an object that looked like a gourd with holes in it.

"Ty, you would like this. It is called a Xun," Hop Sun said. "Listen." He blew into the top hole and with his fingers covered and uncovered the holes near the bottom. It sounded like an owl. He played a melody that was hauntingly beautiful.

"I played this every night after I had worked long hours building the railroad tracks," said Hop Sun. "It gave great comfort to my friends."

Ty could understand that. The mellow tunes made him feel wistful and content. As soon as he mastered the harmonica, he decided that he would learn to play the Xun.

CHAPTER 16: THE BANQUET

To play a harp before a cow
(Throwing pearls before swine)

Mr. Low's restaurant was not doing well. Most of the businesses in Tacoma owned by the Chinese were not doing well. Mr. Low was angry and worried. Before Weisbach had become mayor, the restaurant had flourished. Mr. Low had planned to expand. But now! Mayor Weisbach and his friends were trying to force them out. A true injustice. They had no right to make him leave. Why, he and Mrs. Low had been in Tacoma longer than Mayor Weisbach and most of the townspeople! There must be a solution. He pondered this dilemma as he put clean tablecloths on the tables. He was a worrier by nature and this predicament caused him many sleepless nights. Then he got an idea.

One day after Mrs. Low and Ty finished a game of chess, Mr. Low came into the room. "I have an idea that may help our business," he said. "It may not work but perhaps we should try it. It may help us stay in this town. I can't think of another possibility."

Mrs. Low and Ty looked up at him, curious. He continued, "Mayor Weisbach and his group do not like us and want us gone. We don't like them yet we want to stay. Perhaps if we ate together, we could make peace. We may never be friends but perhaps we could live and work side-by-side. Thus I propose hosting a special banquet here at this restaurant to bring us together. Perhaps we can work out our differences."

Mrs. Low threw her hands in the air. "Eggs should not fight with rocks," she exclaimed.

"What does that mean?" asked Ty, trying to imagine eggs dueling with rocks.

"They could smash us," Mrs. Low said.

"We can't just sit back and accept their treatment," said Mr. Low. "We have to try new strategies. All the merchants will be invited. I will get help from my friends. Mayor Weisbach will not look a gift horse in the mouth."

Ty was perplexed at this horse image.

"The mayor will be invited?" asked Mrs. Low.

"Yes. He needs to get to know us. He will see that we are not so different than he is."

Mrs. Low made a face. "I will feed him spoiled fish and rancid chicken."

"I heard an American saying," Mr. Low said. "It is, 'You can catch more flies with honey than you can with vinegar.'"

Mrs. Low snorted.

Ty was confused. Why would you want to catch flies anyway? He could understand why you would want to kill flies. But catch them? And who would use vinegar?

Mr. Low shook his head when Ty mentioned this. Mrs. Low replied, "Mr. Low believes you'll get a lot further if you're nice than if you're not nice. I'm not so sure."

Why didn't they just say that? Ty thought it was much clearer to say what you mean rather than getting flies involved.

Mrs. Low made a face showing great disdain. "The mayor is as disappointing as an empty dumpling," she said with a sniff.

"Perhaps," said Mr. Low. "But he is a dumpling we cannot ignore."

***

The whole Chinese community helped prepare for the big banquet. Mayor Weisbach declined to attend, saying he was too busy and besides he wasn't partial to that kind of food. But some of the anti-Chinese group sent back word that they would agree to attend.

"Agree to attend," scoffed Mrs. Low. "As if they are doing us a favor. They will be receiving a wonderful free meal. I will glare at each one of them when I see them. My stare will scare them."

Mr. Low had also invited Mrs. Doyle, Eva, Ty, and Li to the banquet. Hop Sun would help serve the food.

"I hope that works out," said Eva a bit dubiously. 'Hop Sun alone could be responsible for destroying any good will between the two groups, if he drops something or trips over a chair or...." They all knew Hop Sun could do most anything.

Ty was excited about going to the banquet. In his entire life, he'd never even gone to something as fancy as church. He was looking forward to eating as much as he wanted. He wasn't sure he'd ever eaten that much.

"This occasion calls for you to take another bath," said Eva. "And remember, Minus is not invited."

"To my bath?" asked Ty.

Eva laughed. "No, to the banquet. He'll have to stay outside."

Ty didn't like to be separated from his dog for any reason, but he figured they both could bear it for a couple of hours, especially if it meant that Minus could have lots of table scraps later.

After the second full bath of his life, Ty dressed in his good clothes and combed his hair for the event. When he was ready, Eva stood back and took a long look at him.

"You are handsome," said Eva. "Look at yourself."

Ty looked into Eva's long mirror and smiled. The boy looking back at him wasn't as scrawny and scared-looking as he used to be. This boy was strong-looking and clean. Ty thought it was fun to get cleaned up. He wouldn't want to do it every day, but it was all right for special occasions. The thought flashed through his head, what if his pa saw him going into the Chinese restaurant? He'd been careful ever since the Fourth of July so that his pa wouldn't see him with Hop Sun, Li, or Mr. Low. In fact Ty tried hard to stay out of his pa's sight all the time. He went days without seeing him or his brothers. Did Pa remember what happened that night? Ty still wasn't sure but he didn't want to take a chance.

Eva, standing in front of her long mirror, tied a green bow in her hair that matched her best dress. Li had borrowed a blue silk dress from

Mrs. Low. "Oh my. You're beautiful," said Eva, impressed. Li blushed and looked proud.

Then they all, including Mrs. Doyle, walked over to Mr. Low's restaurant. Minus was disappointed to have to stay outside, but only for a second. Then he ran off after a cat that dashed in front of him.

As they entered the restaurant, Ty felt again as if he was stepping into another world. Maybe this was like being in China, he thought. Mr. Low had closed the restaurant for outside business as he and his friends prepared for the banquet. They had decorated it elaborately with flowers and colorful banners. Mrs. Low also dressed for the event in her most beautiful black silk dress.

"Confucius says, 'Everything has beauty, but not everyone sees it,'" Mrs. Low said. "I will stay in the office and listen to the festivities. Even though people will not be able to see my complete dress, I will know of its beauty. That is enough."

She stayed on her sofa, but the doors were opened so she could peek out to the restaurant. "I'll be able to relive this night many times in my head," she said. "New memories are welcomed in my well-visited collection of old memories."

***

Ty looked around at the restaurant filled with elegantly-dressed people. The tables were set with white tablecloths and elegant place settings. The Chinese men wore their silk dark tunics. The white men wore dark suits with stiff, high collars. The white women wore long dresses with tight waistlines and sleeves puffed at the shoulder. The Chinese women wore their finest silk dresses with designs of reds, greens, blacks and golds.

Ty glanced down at the women's feet. Mrs. Low was right; the women indeed had tiny feet encased in tiny, pointed shoes. They did not move around easily.

Of course, Chinese was spoken here and there. As Ty listened to the short sounds, long phrases, high pitches dipping into low pitches, his logical mind tried to pick up patterns in their speech. Someday, he thought, he would like to learn Chinese. He walked closer to a group of white men and women talking together, and tried to block out the actual words, to listen to the sounds, the pitches of their conversation in English.

Eva interrupted his game when she pulled him over to look at the food that was being brought out by the Chinese waiters. Hop Sun emerged carrying a big platter of a steaming greens and looking very serious, as if he was concentrating on not tripping.

"Oh my," Eva whispered to Ty. "Doesn't that food look wonderful?" It indeed looked wonderful, and the aroma made Ty's mouth water.

He picked up a menu card which looked like a piece of Chinese art. Eva read the English translation to him:

MENU
Steamed pork with salted fish
Soy sauce steamed pork ribs
Spice duck
Radish fish stew
Tripe and pickled vegetable soup
Boiled greens

Mrs. Doyle, Li, Eva and Ty sat down at their table. Hop Sun came over to them and bowed.

"Everyone is looking very wonderful," Hop Sun said, smiling. "I would like to talk with you, but instead I must work."

He served them their main course. Ty glanced at his plate and saw the salted fish's eyeballs staring up at him.

"Fish eyeballs are delicacies," Li said. "In China, a fish is cooked with the head on – it's a sign of good fortune when heads and tails are left on." Ty wasn't so sure. He'd eaten lots of fish but never the eyeballs.

"When you eat a fish eyeball, keep it in your mouth for as long as possible," Li told him. "Then bite. That way you get the full taste of the fish and the chewy texture. If you swallow too quickly, you won't be able to taste it."

Ty did as she said but he wasn't sure he appreciated the flavor as he should. Because the waiters had not set out spoons, knives or forks, Li showed Ty, Eva and Mrs. Doyle how to make a pinching motion with the chopsticks.

Then from the next table, they heard a pounding on the table. "Waiter! I need regular forks," bellowed one of the white men. "You can't expect me to use those little sticks. Come now. We're civilized here." The other men at the table, all of whom had been vocal against the Chinese, also pounded on their tables. Hop Sun did not look happy but he gave them forks and knives.

Dinner continued, course after delicious course. Ty didn't recognize most of the foods brought out to him but he enjoyed every bite.

After the meal, Mr. Mung, one of the richest Chinese merchants in town, got up to speak. He bowed and then turned to the anti-Chinese group. "We humbly thank you for coming to-night," he said. "We are filled with gratitude that you have honored us so. We sincerely hope our meal has pleased you. We desire that the bonds of friendship and commerce be strengthened between East and West. I toast to you."

He raised his glass of rice brandy. Everyone raised their glasses as well and toasted. Ty looked over at the anti-Chinese table. The white men gulped down their drinks and were whispering to one another, chortling.

Then, from that table, Dr. Chester Winter-mute stood up and raised his glass. "I would like to like to make a toast too. I want to toast Chinese doctors. They rub a tumor with an oyster shell which kills the tumor AND the patient."

The white men laughed. The Chinese men and women looked puzzled.

John Tucker, a grocer, stood up next and raising his glass, said, "Here's to Chinese grocery stores. Where else can you buy dried cat, lizard legs, toasted ants, and all the opium you can smoke?" The white men laughed even louder.

Ty got that bad feeling in his stomach again. He looked around and could see that the Chinese men and women were beginning to understand what was happening: they were being made fun of. But what could they do about it? They sat there, confused.

Then a banker named Joe Dieringer, slightly drunk, pushed himself up from the table and with slurred speech, said, "I salute the Chinese restaurants. They serve the most delicious fric-asseed rat, parboiled mouse, and possum lard sprinkled with insects." The white men pounded the table in appreciation of Joe's humor.

"And now," the banker continued. "Please excuse us. We wish to go home and grow our hair into a braid." The men slapped each other on the back, laughing, and stood up to leave.

At that point, Hop Sun came out, carrying a tray of water glasses. As he got close to the white men who were preparing to leave, Hop Sun stumbled and the water glasses went flying, soaking the men.

They sputtered and shook themselves off. "You fool," said Mr. Tucker to Hop Sun. "You clumsy fool."

Hop Sun tried mopping them up with his apron while talking in Chinese. A Chinese man close to him laughed. Everyone else was stunned. What was Hop Sun saying, Ty wondered.

The white men stormed out angrily, swearing and muttering. The people in the restaurant began talking, greatly agitated. Ty glanced at Mr. Low who looked disappointed and upset. All of his hard work for nothing.

Then Ty looked at Hop Sun who had a grim smile on his face. Ty knew that Hop Sun had not tripped by accident.

"The men should be glad I did not drop the boiling soup on them," said Hop Sun. "Although I did consider it."

"What did you say in Chinese when you dried them off," asked Eva.

"Just that they needed some cooling off," said Hop Sun with a laugh.

Later, after Ty had changed back into his old clothes and was walking home, he thought about the evening. At least he had eaten a wonderful meal. And Mr. Low had given a lot of table scraps to Minus. The dog was trotting next to Ty, his stomach full of wonderful food too.

Whenever you eat a lot of good food, Ty decided, the evening isn't a total loss.

CHAPTER 17: RAMPING UP PRESSURE

Do not fret when the birds of worry
fly over your head;
just don't let them build nests in your hair.

Mr. Rowland's grocery store on Pacific was the first to cave in to the boycott. When business suffered, Mr. Rowland fired his Chinese workers and took out an ad in the Ledger to show his change of heart:

The CHINESE

Must Go!

So Say

W. G. Rowland & Co.

If they are still employed, how can they go?

Turn Them Off!

Do not employ them; by so doing you will drive them out.

They Must Go

So say all of us; but read our ad first.

Eastern Syrup, gal....65 cents

California Bacon....11 cents

Fresh Ranch Butter....65 cents

English Breakfast Tea...50 cents

Mr. Rowland was philosophical about his decision. "The Chinese are good workers, but I won't be able to feed my own family if I have to close my business. I have no loyalty to the Chinese. Every man for himself, that's what I always say. I'm sure the Chinese would say the same thing."

The anti-Chinese were increasing pressure on Mrs. Doyle too. One evening two large men, one with a big brown beard and the other with a long scar on his face, came by the house to demand once again that Li leave.

"Who are you anyway?" Mrs. Doyle said.

"Friends of Tacoma," said the man with the scar. "Get rid of the Chinese woman."

"Please go," Mrs. Doyle said, shutting the door.

"We warned you. Remember that," the bearded man yelled from outside. "You have been warned!"

Two nights later when Mrs. Doyle, Eva and Li returned from a walk, they saw the windows of their house were smashed. The door had been forced open. Someone had broken in.

Cautiously Mrs. Doyle pushed open the door.

"Hello?" called out Mrs. Doyle. Silence. She picked up a fire poker and started to walk

through the house. Chairs were turned over, curtains torn down, drawers pulled out and the con-
tents dumped on the floor. Nothing was taken,
but damage was done. Eva and Li stayed in the
bedroom, picking up items while Mrs. Doyle
went to the parlor.

She gave a little gasp when she opened the
door. There, on the floor, was her typewriter,
smashed into pieces. Tears came to her eyes.

It was just a typewriter, she told herself, just
a machine. But she knew in her heart it was
more than that. For one thing, she had used all
of her money to buy it. It provided her with an
income. It was keeping the three of them from
starving. That machine also kept her from having to return to New York. When she left, she'd
taken only the money that was hers, nothing
more. No jewelry, no valuables, none of her husband's money. She had just enough to buy the
typewriter and two train tickets. She'd been furious with her husband for putting people in
danger, for not getting help when she'd asked.
She wanted to get as far away as possible.

If her parents were alive, they would have
helped her. But they weren't, and now, looking
at the broken typewriter and the broken win-

dows, she realized no one would help her. Suddenly she felt totally defeated. That was it. She couldn't go on. How could she stand up to this pressure? How could she live in such a town? How would she make a living now? She still had to feed herself, her daughter, and Li. She felt helpless and hopeless. Instinctively she bent over and started picking up the pieces of the broken typewriter.

When Eva came into the office a few minutes later, she saw her grim-looking mother placing the pieces on the desk.

"What are we going to do?" asked Eva. Li took out the broom and began sweeping up the shattered glass from the broken windows.

Mrs. Doyle looked at her daughter wearily. "I have no idea," she said. "So for now we'll bolt the door, and we'll go to bed. The Christian response is to forgive. That's not what I'm feeling now."

Eva gulped. Her mother always knew what to do. Well, something would work out. Isn't that what Hop Sun always said? She surely hoped Hop Sun was right.

***

The next morning when Mrs. oyle, Eva, and Li were eating their breakfast, they heard a knock on the door. There stood Ty and Minus, looking hopeful. Ty grinned at them shyly.

Mrs. Doyle sighed. Two more mouths to feed. Still, she managed a smile for the boy and dog. "Hungry?" she asked. "Come on in. There's always room for one-or two- more."

Ty took a step into the house and then he saw the broken windows. He glanced in the parlor and saw the pieces of the typewriter.

"Oh no," he said softly. "What happened?"

"Someone broke in here last night and smashed everything," said Eva. "I'd like to get my hands on them. I'd fix them."

"Me too," said Mrs. Doyle. "They'd be surprised at how fierce we Doyle women are when we're mad."

"Can you repair the typewriter?" asked Ty.

"I don't know," said Mrs. Doyle. "I'm not good at that sort of thing."

When she glanced at Ty, she saw he had a glimmer in his eye. "I like machines," he said. "I like fixing things."

"You can try," said Mrs. Doyle. "But first eat something."

Ty sat down at the table, quickly ate, and then got to work.

"You have another gift, don't you?" said Eva, watching him lay out all the pieces and with a pencil and paper, draw a sketch of what it should look like inside.

He then proceeded to see if it would go together again. The fall to the ground had bent some of the pieces. Ty had to twist them and experiment with putting them into place, but slowly the typewriter took shape.

"All the King's horses and all the King's men couldn't put Humpty Dumpty together again," said Eva as he worked. "But Ty could."

By lunchtime, Ty had assembled the typewriter. It looked a little bent and misshapen, but it worked.

Mrs. Doyle only hoped that enough of her customers would use her services so she could still make a living. She would have to wait and see. She could use a bit of luck right about now. Good luck, that is.

***

Later that week, a Chinese man they didn't know stumbled into Mr. Low's restaurant, dirty, hungry, and exhausted. "I was attacked," he said, "Two days ago. Outside Seattle."

Mr. Low sat the man at a table and brought him tea and some food.

"My friends were killed!" the man said. "The hop farmers hired Chinese pickers. We were willing to work for less than the white and Indian workers. But the white men and Indians got angry and came back to the farm and shot into the tent where we were sleeping."

He covered his face with his hands in anguish.

***

A week later, more disturbing news came. Eva read Ty the headlines in the newspaper:

Twenty-eight Chinese Massacred in Rock Springs Mining Town!

One hundred and fifty white miners in Rock Springs, Wyoming, attack Chinese miners, killing 28 and wounding 15 others.

Several hundred other Chinese driven out of town.

Eva turned to look at Ty with wide eyes. "Remember when Hop Sun came on that boat with the other Chinese men from Canada?" she said. "Those men went on to Wyoming."

Ty knew what she was thinking. The men could have ended up at Rock Springs. Possibly they had been slaughtered. Hop Sun could have been killed too. A massacre in a far-off state suddenly became very close.

When Mrs. Low heard this, she looked at her husband in alarm. "Should we leave too?" she asked. "It feels dangerous."

"We can't leave now," said Mr. Low. "Think of all that we have invested here."

"But they may kill us here," said Mrs. Low. "I am not going to squander all those months of lying here on this couch just to be killed by these hateful townspeople. What a waste of all that reclining."

"This is the United States of America," Mr. Low said. "We are protected. There are laws." He did not look hopeful.

Ty knew there were laws, he just wasn't sure anyone in town enforced the laws.

CHAPTER 18: CHURCH

The summer insect doubts the existence of ice.

The Presbyterian minister, Rev. McFarland, now carried two Colt revolvers strapped around his waist. It started after three men came to his house and told his wife to fire their Chinese servants or their family "would not be safe." Rev. McFarland was furious. "I have no servants. I'm a minister, I'm too poor," he told people. "But everyone had better come to church this Sunday. I have a few things to say."

***

Ty had never been to church, but Eva convinced him he'd better come that Sunday. "It may be extremely entertaining to hear Rev. McFarland's sermon," she said.

So on Sunday, Ty ran down the hill to Eva's house where Eva and her mother were waiting for him, dressed in their Sunday best. He scrubbed himself with soap and water, got into his good set of clothes too, and they set off to the Presbyterian church.

"I have never looked forward to church with such anticipation," said Eva happily.

Other people must have felt the same way. The church was packed. The organist, a frail-looking woman, played hymns as everyone got settled. The little Presbyterian church was filled with people of all denominations – Catholics, Unitarians, and Lutherans. And too, there were people who hadn't been in any church for years who just wanted to see what sort of fireworks would erupt that day.

Ty was fascinated by the pipe organ. How did it work? How could the organist play the keyboard and pedals and the sounds come out the pipes? Then she started playing, "Amazing Grace." Everyone began singing:

Amazing grace!
How sweet the sound,
That saved a wretch, like me!
I once was lost, but now am found,
Was blind, but now I see.

Rev. McFarland strode up to the pulpit, his long gown flowing, with fury in his eye. "Today I will talk about Christian love," he said, looking at his parishioners sternly. "Love our neighbors as ourselves. Have you ever heard that before?" He looked expectantly out at the congregation. People waited for him to go on. "Did the Good Book say, only love them if they look like us? If their eyes are shaped like ours? If they worship like we do? Eat like we do? Do everything exactly like we do? NO! I tell you, NO!" He slammed his hand down on the pulpit and glared. "And who of you remembers what Jesus said in the book of Luke: Do unto others as you would have them do unto you. Did Jesus say EXCEPT the Chinese? Well? Did he?"

People in the congregation murmured and muttered.

Rev. McFarland continued: "We pastors are under oath to speak for God. If this community fails to take sides against the wrong, we have not done our job. We must bring the gospel to bear directly on this issue. If evil is here, we must stop it. NOW."

Eva, who'd been on the edge of her seat, now stood up and started clapping. Her eyes were shining. "Bravo!" she cried. Other people started applauding as well.

One man stood up and angrily shouted, "You don't understand the problem!"

Another yelled, "The Chinese are the evil ones!" Two men made a big show of getting up and walking out of the church. Their wives and children scurried out behind them, mortified.

Rev. McFarland's face got very red. He shouted after them, "Go! Go! I will preach on till the benches are empty!"

The organist started to play "Rock of Ages" but no one sang. The sanctuary was filled with excited people, arguing and yelling. A couple of the men started shoving, and when they got outside, fists started flying.

Ty and Eva ran outside too, but they didn't want to see the fighting. As they tried to decide which way to get around the fights, they overheard one man behind them say to another, "We've got to work harder to get rid of the Chinese."

"I think we can do it without anyone getting hurt," said the other. "We don't want to hurt anyone."

"Right," said the first man. "We still have many legal options. At our next meeting, I'm going to propose that the city do a health risk assessment of the Chinese. The sanitary conditions are horrible."

The man looked at his friend. "What are you talking about? They're extremely clean."

The first man smiled. "We'll see..." And they walked off.

Eva and Ty looked at each other. "They're going to find all sorts of unsanitary conditions," said Eva.

"They'd lie?" asked Ty, puzzled.

"Yes," said Eva. "As long as they get people mad about the Chinese, they'd lie. We have to let someone know what they're planning to do."

"Let's tell Hop Sun," said Ty.

They ran to the laundry to try to find Hop Sun and found him sitting with Li outside the laundry watching people go by. On his one day off a week, Hop Sun liked to relax in the morning and walk down to the waterfront after lunch. Lately, it seemed, Li joined him.

Breathlessly, Eva told him what they'd heard. He just smiled his wide smile. "Then we will make sure everything is extra clean and tidy. We will keep one step ahead of them."

That strategy would have worked, Ty later thought, if the anti-Chinese had played fair. But they didn't. As planned, later that week Mayor Weisbach commissioned a health study on the conditions of the Chinese establishments. When Eva and Ty heard that, Eva got another of her ideas.

"Just for fun, let's find out where the people doing the study are going, and see exactly how they're conducting the study," she suggested.

The two men who were tasked with the health study were irritated to find a red-headed girl, a small boy, and his three-legged dog everywhere they went. As they were taking down information, Eva, too, was writing in her notebook. They went to five laundries, three restaurants, four grocery stores, the bunkhouse, and several homes of Chinese merchants. Hop Sun had spread the word and every place sparkled with cleanliness.

Hop Sun was happy at how his warning had motivated the best conditions ever seen in any of the establishments. "There wasn't one thing found that was out of place or dirty," he said to Eva. Eva and Ty agreed.

But they should have known that the two men would not report the truth.

The newspaper published their report: "Houses are stacked from floor to ceiling with bunks, and men, women and children were sleeping in these horrid conditions. The Chinese disregard boundaries and build their shacks on public property. Their laundries are filthy, with suds running out into the street. Chinese laundrymen rinse clothes in dirty water. The Chinese slaughter pigs in cruel and inhumane ways, torturing them in the process."

When the citizens of Tacoma read about these made-up but scary-sounding conditions in the newspapers, they were appalled. More townspeople felt the Chinese should leave. Eva spent a day writing a letter to the newspaper telling them the truth, but the newspaper did not publish her letter.

Then one day, while Ty and Mrs. Low were playing chess, Mr. Low came into the office waving the newspaper in great agitation. "Listen," he said. "The grand jury investigating the Rock Springs, Wyoming, massacre refused to bring the murderers to trial, claiming no witnesses will testify. The murderers returned to their homes, celebrated as heroes by the townspeople. Heroes!"

He shook his head in disbelief. "They have gotten away with murder."

Mrs. Low gently put her hand on his hand and said, "The trees want to remain quiet, but the wind will not stop." She looked at Ty. "Even though we want peace, trouble is brewing."

Ty got that familiar shaky feeling in the pit of his stomach again. Something bad was going to happen.

CHAPTER 19: BACK TO SCHOOL

One chirp surprises everyone.
(Discovering an unknown talent)

In early September, school started again. Whereas Miss Shaw, their teacher from the year before was a big exuberant woman, this year's teacher, Mr. Abner, was as dry as an old piece of driftwood. He was tall and spindly with gray teeth, papery pale skin, and wispy white hair. His eyes bulged behind round wire glasses.

"I pride myself on being rational," he intoned in a flat and monotone voice, which perfectly suited his flat, dull appearance. "I examine the facts and come to conclusions that merit attention." Sometimes his sentences didn't even make sense, according to Eva, but he said them with such certainty that they sounded like they made sense, especially when he gave his opinions about the Chinese.

"Class, as I am, and have been, a teacher of the young for forty years or more, I will tell you the facts, as I have learned them," he droned one day. "The Chinese people are unlike good Christian folk. They are without emotion." (Here Eva felt like laughing since Mr. Abner said it in a perfect monotone.)

"They descend from a barbaric people who, over the course of centuries have a tendency to act in problematic ways. They are hardworking, I grant them that. But their morals are not our morals. Their ways are not our ways. I am only telling you the facts. Their customs are different. They value saving face, above all else. If that means they must lie, so be it. But when you cannot count on a person's statements to be true, the whole basis for a rational society is gone. I have nothing against any people, but all races were given land by the Good Lord and they need to return to the land that God has given them."

Eva raised her hand. "What about the Puyallup Indians?" she asked. "God gave them this land and now we live here," she said.

Mr. Abner smiled, his thin dry lips stretching just a bit, but his eyes didn't smile. "The native tribes never settled one particular place. They were nomadic thus this area was wide open for those European settlers who felt the sting of prejudice in their own country."

At recess, though, Ty and Eva heard some of the girls talking. "I didn't know what to think before," Becky said. "But Mr. Abner gave us facts. How can you argue with the facts?"

Eva walked over to the group of girls, a fierce and determined expression on her face. "I'll tell you some facts," she said, her voice rising. When she got excited all of her theatrical tendencies came out. "What facts would you like to know? Almost everyone in this country except the Indians came from someplace else. My father's family came from England, my mother's family from Ireland."

"Mine came from Sweden," said Elsa.

Becky looked thoughtful. "Mine came from France."

"Mayor Weisbach himself came from Germany," said Eva. "My friend Mr. Low from China speaks English better than he does. What right does Mayor Weisbach have to tell my friends to leave?"

"You know the Chinese are heathens," said Rachel, her eyes serious. "They don't believe in God."

"Oh, they believe in God. They just call God a different name," said Eva.

Rachel looked confused. "Well, my aunt told me that last month she was trying to teach the

Chinese about our God at her house. Mrs. Snodgrass came to pay a visit, and as she came up the walkway, she said she looked in the window and saw that the Chinese were making faces at my aunt behind her back. Isn't that rude?"

Ty came over to Eva then and whispered in her ear. Eva smiled. Then she turned to the girls. "Ty says that if Mrs. Snodgrass could see the Chinese through the window, the Chinese could also see her. Why would they make faces then? That just doesn't add up."

"Well, what about those braids all the men wear?" asked Rachel. "If they want to fit in here, why don't they cut their braid? Braids are for girls."

Ty started to whisper in Eva's ear again, but Eva looked at him and said, "Don't tell me, Ty. Tell them."

Ty looked down at the ground but he knew he had to tell them what Hop Sun had told him earlier. "The rulers of China say they will behead any Chinese man who doesn't have a braid," Ty said in a low voice. "The Chinese men here can be turned out of our country at any point. They can't grow a braid in the time it takes to return by ship to China. So they have to keep their braid."

196

Rachel smiled at Ty. "Thank you for explaining that," she said. Eva beamed at him like a proud mother.

"Well, why are there hardly any Chinese women in town?" asked a girl named Emily. "There are so many men, and they cram together in those bunk houses. Mother says it's not natural."

Eva shook her head in disgust. "Our government won't allow Chinese women to come to the United States unless they're already married to men of wealth. Mrs. Low could come because Mr. Low was a merchant. Of course, some Chinese women are smuggled into our country by bad men in order to be prostitutes. Our government looks the other way when this happens."

The girls looked shocked. Eva wasn't through, though. "Also, it's against the law in the United States for Chinese men to marry white women. So what are they supposed to do? How can they ever marry here? Most of them hope to make enough money to return to China and get married there."

She continued her eloquent defense of the Chinese and by the end of the recess, all of the girls were excited to learn about the Chinese culture and perhaps even take a field trip to Mr. Low's restaurant to sample the cuisine.

When they returned to the classroom Becky said to Mr. Abner, "None of us girls agree with your opinions of the Chinese now. Eva set us straight."

Mr. Abner decided right then that he did not like the smarty-pants red-haired girl. She was much too big for her britches.

***

Mr. Abner had been warned by the old teacher Miss Shaw that the shabby, dirty boy named Tyrus – a friend to the smug redheaded girl – could not read. "Probably a lazy child," Mr. Abner thought. "Perhaps with an inferior brain as well." He prided himself on his own intellect. God had not blessed him with good looks or athletic abilities but he was given a sharp brain. In fact, in his opinion, he should have been teaching in a more prestigious school; perhaps a college would be more fitting for his gifts.

That afternoon Mr. Abner, still smarting from Becky's comment, decided that while he couldn't get back at the redheaded girl, he could get some satisfaction exposing her dimwitted friend.

"This afternoon, class, we will have a reading assessment," Mr. Abner announced. "I have my suspicions that some of you should repeat your former grade due to your lack of skills. You, Tyrus Ritter, come up here." Smiling his dry, tight smile, Mr. Abner picked up his long ruler and pointed to Ty. Ty's eyes got wide with alarm, which Mr. Abner noted with satisfaction. Ty slowly walked up to the front of the class, his face red.

Mr. Abner wrote something on the chalkboard. "Read this," Mr. Abner ordered Ty. Ty felt his mouth go dry. He shook his head.

"No?" said Mr. Abner. "You refuse?"

Someone in the class snickered. Mr. Abner wrote something else on the chalkboard. "Read this then," he said.

Ty looked up and tried to figure out the words. At Mrs. Doyle's house, he could read simple sentences. But now, standing in front of the whole class with a teacher holding a long ruler, he looked at the chalkboard and his mind was swirling so he just couldn't read. Besides, he was used to the way a typewriter made letters. The 'a' of a typewriter didn't look like one Mr. Abner made. Ty looked miserably down at the floor.

Just then Eva jumped up and said, "It says 'Read this or face the consequences.'"

Mr. Abner turned to her, furious. "I wanted him to read it, not you. Would you like to take this instead of him too?" Mr. Abner said, holding up the ruler.

Eva looked at him, almost bemused. "No, you will not be hitting either of us," she said. "Corporal punishment is against the constitution of the United States. The Eighth Amendment of the United States Constitution prohibits you from imposing cruel and unusual punishment. If anyone is struck, I assure you that my mother will speak to the superintendent. I believe you are already on probation, so this would not look good."

All of the students looked at Eva, shocked. Was this true? How did she know that information about the teacher?

Mr. Abner pale white skin flushed a deep purple. "I...I...I..." He couldn't think of what to say.

He swallowed, and his Adam's apple bounced up and down. He felt uneasy. What if this know-it-all girl was telling the truth? Was he on probation? He had gotten a poor review last year due to complaints from some parents. He started to perspire.

Then Eva looked around the room proudly. "Ty is just now learning how to read. However, he happens to be a mathematical genius," she announced. Mr. Abner came back to reality with that statement and gave a snide, derisive laugh. "You don't believe me?" Eva asked. "Ty would like to challenge you to a chess game, Mr. Abner."

Mr. Abner looked startled, then a sly smile crept over his face.

This smug girl had embarrassed him. But chess! Mr. Abner prided himself on his chess ability. This dull boy would be no intellectual match in the game Mr. Abner studied every night. Chess was his passion.

"I happen to have a chess board right here," said Mr. Abner, hoping that his easy victory would allow him to regain the respect of his class. He wanted to show that little brat and the rest of this class just how smart he was.

He brought out his board and set it up on his desk. Ty came around to the other side and Eva pulled up a chair for him. For a second, when Mr. Abner caught a glimpse of the intense focus of Ty's eyes, he got a little scared. What if this urchin really did know how to play chess? Preposterous. He'd make short work out of this pathetic lad.

Mr. Abner picked up his pawn and moved it to the center of the board. Ty immediately attacked the pawn with his knight.

Mr. Abner smiled. "Let me educate you, children," he said out loud to the whole class. He would now teach the class what a true chess player thinks about when playing the game. They could learn from him, the master of the game. He cleared his throat and said, "I took the center in my opening move. If our little friend here had a bit more experience, he'd know he should never have made his knight so vulnerable. Ah, but he will find out soon."

Ty didn't change expression. He frowned with a single-minded concentration that Mr. Abner again found a bit unnerving.

Ten minutes later, the game was over. "Checkmate," Ty said quietly. He had not yelled it or sounded the least bit triumphant, but the words cut right into Mr. Abner's heart.

Eva shouted, "Ty beat Mr. Abner!" A low buzz filled the room.

Mr. Abner had no idea what had happened. The little urchin had had a stroke of luck. It was a fluke. "Beginner's luck," said Mr. Abner, flus-tered. "We shall have a rematch."

Two more games later, Mr. Abner and the whole class knew that Ty's wins were not flukes.

Never had Mr. Abner seen the moves that Ty had used. The teacher was humiliated and furi-ous that this boy had made a mockery of him.

"Enough of this nonsense," said Mr. Abner, his face splotchy red with embarrassment. "We shall resume our class."

Ty, flushed with victory, walked back to his seat; this time, his head was held high. All of the other students looked at him with admiration. Eva beamed proudly.

That day after school, Edward Pederson and Michael O'Flannery, two of the smarter boys in the class, asked Ty to teach them chess. Kristin Snesrud ran up to Ty too and told him that she played. "Perhaps we can play each other now and then," she said with excitement. "My father can't keep up to me anymore."

Ty shyly agreed to teaching and playing. He was embarrassed at the attention but felt tickled in a way. When you have friends, he thought, school might actually be fun.

CHAPTER 20: FINDING THE TRUNK
Paper cannot wrap up a fire.
(The truth cannot be concealed)

One day at the end of September Angel gave Ty a most wonderful surprise. The cat had been chasing a mouse in the barn and had followed it into the far corner, digging through decaying hay in pursuit. The mouse scurried out, Angel followed, the hay shifted, and there – exposed – was a battered old trunk. His pa must have tossed it there when they moved to Tacoma. Rain had seeped through one end, and a mouse or two had gnawed at the corners.

"Buried treasure!" Ty said as he uncovered the whole trunk. He opened it and pulled out two old cookbooks, an ancient Bible, a wooden jewelry box, and a photo of his pa with a woman. Was she his ma? Neither of them were smiling. His pa, bearded and young, looked defiantly at the camera, and the woman looked slightly off to the left, with sad eyes. It appeared as if she was pregnant. He turned the photograph over and read the two names printed: Zeke and Laura Ritter. It *was* his ma. Laura was her name. Ty was startled to see that she, like his pa, was tall and blonde. He'd always assumed she was small and dark, like he was. Ty stared at the woman for a long time. He sure wished he could remember even a little bit of what she was like.

Then he opened the wooden jewelry box and saw a brooch, a gold cross on a chain, and a small leather-bound book, which had some handwritten numbers, perhaps birthdates of people his mother knew.

As he set the wooden box back into the trunk, he noticed something: the box looked like it had a false bottom. The inside bottom of the box was higher than the outside. He knocked on that space with his knuckle, and it sounded hollow. He pushed on the sides, and sure enough, the bottom slid open, revealing a secret drawer. Inside was a package of letters tied with a string. Unfortunately, they were written in cursive. Tucking the letters into his pants pocket, Ty decided he'd take them to Eva. If she'd read them to him, he might learn something about his ma. Who was this woman who gave birth to him and then died a short time later?

***

When Ty brought the letters down to Eva, she gave him some breakfast and then carefully untied the letters.

"Who are they to?" asked Ty, sitting on the edge of his chair, chewing his bread.

"Laura Ritter," said Eva, reading the envelope. "But they weren't mailed through the post office. There isn't a stamp."

"Laura Ritter is my ma," said Ty.

"Let's see here," said Eva, opening one of the letters. "It says 'Dearest Laura...'"

Eva scanned the letter quickly and frowned. "What's your father's name?" she asked.

"Zeke."

Eva looked up at Ty and then looked back down at the letter. "This is from a man named Matthew. The date indicates it's about twelve years ago."

Ty did a quick calculation. "I'm eleven and seven twelfths," he said.

Eva cleared her throat and proceeded to read. **"Dearest Laura, I didn't see you today at the store, so I am writing this letter to inquire about your health. I hope your husband has not found out about us. I am afraid of what he will do to you. In two months' time I will have saved enough money so we can leave together. You need never see that despicable man again. I hope you will come to the store tomorrow. Yours forever, Matthew."**

206

Ty blinked. What did that letter mean?

Eva slid the second of the three letters out of its envelope. **"My dearest, We have made plans and must hope that all will work out. We must leave before the baby is born. I know you are trying to get things ready for your departure. I am convinced that your very life is at risk. We must leave soon. One week seems like forever. Until then, my love, I remain yours forever, Matthew."**

Eva opened the final envelope. Two twenty-dollar bills fluttered out. Eva looked at them in surprise and then she read the last note.

"My Own,

I write this in haste. Enclosed is money for your trip. I will meet you and your sons in Minneapolis three days from today. All my love, M."

Eva slid the final note back into its envelope. Slowly she picked up the money.

"Why didn't she meet him?" Eva asked.

Then she looked at a newspaper clipping that was tucked in between the envelopes. It was an obituary.

MATTHEW   PORTER   KILLED   BY FALLING BARN

"On Wednesday morning Matthew Porter who resides in Lost Prairie, went to the barn immediately after breakfast to feed his hens. The

barn had been raised up and stood upon a temporary underpinning. Mr. Porter went under the barn to feed the hens and while there, a portion of the underpinning gave way and the barn fell upon him, killing him instantly. Mr. Porter was a respected citizen and had been employed at Schmidt's Jewelry Store where he repaired watches and jewelry. He was a gentleman of rare mental endowment, at least in one direction. He was a man of great originality and inventive faculty. He was one of the very small number of men who keep shoving the world along in spite of its slowness and stupidity by the sheer force of their genius. He, for instance, could not only make watches, chronometers, and other like delicate mechanical contrivances, but he made the tools with which they were made. We are also informed that everything he did, he did well. He was 36 years old at the time of his death and leaves no survivors."

"He might have left one survivor," said Eva slowly. "He died one month before you were born. You were the baby he was referring to." They were both quiet, thinking.

"You think he was my pa?" asked Ty breaking the silence.

"I don't know," said Eva.

"Pa knows," said Ty.

Eva looked at him, surprised. "Why do you say that?"

Ty didn't say anything. But now it made sense to him. That was the reason Ty didn't resemble his brothers or his pa. Brown hair, not blonde. Brown eyes, not blue. Slight build, not stocky. His pa could easily have seen that.

Eva held out the forty dollars to Ty. "This is yours," she said. "Given to your mother. Obviously, the man you call your father hadn't read these letters or he would have taken this money. What are you going to do with it?"

Ty looked down at the bills. His mother had meant to take that money and escape, but she never had time. What would he do with it? He could buy food, he always needed food. He could buy clothes. Probably, though, he'd save it. You never know when it would come in handy. And it was comforting to him to know that someone who had loved his mother had touched those bills. His mother must have held those bills too. She just didn't have time to use them. For now, Ty thought, he'd save the money.

Ty was thankful the trunk had not been thrown away when they moved from Minnesota to Washington. He was thankful too that he slept out in the barn. Otherwise, he would never have known about the letters and the story of his parents. As Li would say, it was Fate.

CHAPTER 21: THE WEDDING

I will hold your hand
and be together with you until we're old.

Mr. Malachi Hill, Mrs. Doyle's landlord came to their house one afternoon and stood at the doorway looking nervous.

"Well, uh, Mrs. Doyle," he said. "Uh, this isn't easy to say, but the Chinese girl can't stay in the house anymore."

"Why?" asked Mrs. Doyle. She had one hand on her hip. She'd been afraid of something like this.

"Well, uh, people are putting pressure on me not to rent to you," said Mr. Hill, shifting his weight from side to side.

"Are you so spineless and weak that you can't withstand pressure?" Mrs. Doyle asked.

"Not weak. Practical. I can't afford to make people mad." Mr. Hill's face was red.

"Ah, but you will make me mad," Mrs. Doyle said.

"You, I can afford to make mad," Mr. Hill said. "But I got a lot of other business dealings I can't afford to lose. So either the girl goes, or you all go. You'd best think about it."

Then he left.

Li was in the kitchen and heard the two talking. She knew that Mrs. Doyle couldn't afford to rent another house. She knew too that the food she ate took precious money, money that Mrs. Doyle didn't have.

"If I move to another town, Kaw Chung can come back and get me," Li thought. "The next town may send me back. I have no money. My arm does not straighten and it may never fully be useful."

If she made it to Canada, would things be easier? Perhaps. But how could she get there? And what would she do to support herself?

Li paced in the kitchen. She hadn't told Mrs. Doyle this but Hai Lum, a plump, sweaty, middle-aged Chinese man who owned a grocery store, had been trying to court her. He'd watch for her as she went out walking and would leer at her and tell her how much he wanted to marry her.

She did not like him. He was rich but he was a vulture. Besides, she heard he had a wife back in China.

Now Li looked at her right arm and anger rose within her. With two strong arms, she wouldn't need to rely on anyone. She could work.

She could make it to Canada and survive. But with one useless arm, she was no good to anyone, except perhaps, a leering old man who thought she was weak and desperate.

Well, she thought, her body might be weak but her resolve was not. She would move to Canada and hope for the best. She would leave as soon as she could make arrangements.

That day Hop Sun, however, came to visit her. His usual smile was gone, and he was agitated. "I have heard Hai Lum bragging about how you will marry him," he said.

"No," said Li. "I would rather jump in the middle of the ocean than marry him. But I must move to Canada. I will find work there, even with one arm. I am clever."

"If you were to marry me, I could take care of you," Hop Sun said.

Li looked at him. "I do not wish for anyone to take care of me," she said. "I am strong. I will survive."

"We could take care of each other," said Hop Sun.

Li paused, many thoughts going through her head. "I may be a weight around your neck," she said. "A weight that will sink us both."

Hop Sun smiled. "I think together we will float."

"I will consider this," she said, thinking

Hop Sun nodded. "I have hope," he said and smiled again. "Everything will work out."

Later that evening, Li accepted his offer.
***

The next day Hop Sun came over to the Doyles' house to tell Mrs. Doyle, Eva and Ty the news. They, along with Li, were in the parlor, listening to Mrs. Doyle play the piano.

"Li and I are going to be married," said Hop Sun, smiling.

"Married! Well!" said Mrs. Doyle, surprised. "Tell us about it."

"Being blown up at the factory was the best thing to happen to me," said Hop Sun. "That is how I got Li to see me."

"Yes, that is true. You were hard to miss, covered with blood," Li said.

Hop Sun beamed. "You see?" he said. "It softened her heart. Even being injured can mean happiness in the long run. Everything works out."

"My arm keeps me from being independent now," said Li. "But I will figure out how to work. We will work together."

"So where and when you will be married?" asked Mrs. Doyle.

"We hope that Mr. and Mrs. Low will allow the ceremony to be in the restaurant," Hop Sun said. "And as soon as possible."

Ty looked over at Eva, expecting her to be smiling and happy for the couple. She loved romance and drama. She loved both Li and Hop Sun. Instead he was surprised to see her frowning. Wasn't she excited for them? She didn't seem thrilled at all.

After Hop Sun and Li left to talk to Mr. and Mrs. Low, Eva explained her reaction to him.

"Hop Sun is one of the nicest men I know," she said. "Yet it doesn't seem right that Li should have to marry him because she has no other choice. Is she just being sold again? "

When Li came home later, Eva decided to talk to her. "Do you really want to get married?" Eva asked. "Or are you being forced to?"

Li sat with Ty and Eva at the kitchen table. "I have no family here," she said. "Your mother has been generous but I can't keep taking from her. I can't return to China. I have no money to buy a ticket and besides, what would I do there? My family is very very poor. And I have a damaged arm."

"And big feet," said Ty, remembering what Mrs. Low had told him.

Li laughed. "Yes, big feet. Useless arm and big feet, but still Hop Sun wants to marry me."

"Do you love Hop Sun?" Eva asked her.

Li looked at Eva, puzzled. "In my country, marriages are arranged by the parents. Husband and wife often do not meet until the day of the wedding. They cannot say yes or no."

Eva was confused. "But..."

"I want to survive," Li said. "But I also want to be happy. I will not marry Hai Lum. I do not like him. Hop Sun is a good man. I like him. We will have a good life."

Eva pondered this. "Here, couples mostly marry for love, but sometimes they also marry for other reasons," she said. "I heard of a widow with six small children who married a much older man so she could keep her family together. I also heard of a man who proposed to a woman so they could have twice the amount of land to homestead."

"Hop Sun and I will be strong together," Li said. And they all believed that was true.

***

Mrs. Low was thrilled to host the wedding at the restaurant. She insisted on loaning Li another of her dresses, a beautiful red silk dress – which symbolized joy – traditional in Chinese weddings.

"Planning a wedding will give me hours of entertainment," she told Ty after they played their daily game of chess. "This will get me through another week since I seem to be powerless to make time go by faster. As the proverb says, "You cannot pull the seedlings to help them grow."

Immediately she began organizing. No detail was too small for Mrs. Low to obsess over. Poor Mr. Low shook his head. "I will have no peace until this wedding is over! Woe is me." Mrs. Low just laughed at him.

On the night before the wedding, the couple and their friends gathered in Mrs. Low's office for the traditional hair combing ceremony. Candles were placed around the office; their flickering light gave the room a warm glow and a cozy, intimate feeling.

Hop Sun and Li came into the room and sat in front of an open window. Outside the moon was visible.

To begin the pre-wedding ceremony, Li knelt in front of Mrs. Low who remained reclining on the couch. Mrs. Low took a delicate silver comb and combed Li's hair four times.

"We ask blessings that you be together to the end," Mrs. Low said, smiling at her young friend. "We ask blessings for a hundred years of harmony in your marriage. We ask that you be blessed with a houseful of children and grandchildren. And we ask that the two of you be blessed with long lives."

Then Mr. Low held up a bowl of a sweet dessert soup with pink little dumplings. "Eat this in order to have a complete and sweet marriage," he said.

Mr. Low presented gifts to Hop Sun as Li's dowry since her parents weren't able to do so.

First, Mr. Low held up a pair of scissors and a ruler and said, "Hop Sun, we give you scissors to represent that you and Li are two butterflies never separating. We give you rulers in hopes that you will acquire acres of fields." Then he pointed to the other objects on the table. "We give you this vase for you to attain peace and wealth. Finally, we give you a sewing basket, a tea set, and two pairs of red wedding slippers."

Hop Sun bowed to Mrs. Low and then Mr. Low. Eva read a poem that Mrs. Low had translated:

Oath of Friendship
Anon.,China (1st Century B.C.)

I want to be your friend
Forever and ever without break or decay.
When the hills are all flat
And the rivers are all dry,
When it thunders in winter,
When it snows in summer,
When Heaven and Earth mingle
Not 'til then will I part from you.
***

The morning of the wedding dawned overcast and cool, but to Ty it was the most beautiful day ever. He'd never been to a wedding. He especially looked forward to the banquet after the ceremony. Once again, he ran down to Eva's house, washed up, and then dressed in his good clothes. He even combed his hair. He was getting used to these fancy occasions. He was tickled that even Minus was invited. Eva tied a red bow around the dog's neck.

Li wore Mrs. Low's red silk dress and the red wedding slippers. She walked with Mrs. Doyle,

Eva, Ty, and Minus the three blocks to the restaurant.

As the little group neared their destination, a few young Chinese men along the street lit firecrackers in celebration.

"It is our custom," said Li after they'd passed the men. Minus barked frantically at the little explosions but Ty secretly would have liked to have thrown a few firecrackers too.

A red banner hung across the front doors of the restaurant. They entered and saw a red carpet on the floor which led into the office where the wedding was to take place.

Hop Sun entered the office wearing a red robe. The wedding ceremony was simple. The Chinese priest stood in front of a makeshift altar on which was placed a bowl of fruit and two candles. Mr. Low lit two sticks of incense and placed them by the candles which he also lit. Hop Sun and Li walked to the altar and bowed three times, once to honor Heaven and Earth, once to honor their family ancestors, and finally once to honor each other. The priest said the official words of marriage and then asked, "Do you wish to be married?"

"Yes, we wish to be married," said Hop Sun and Li said together. And it was over. They were married.

Eva read another poem that Mrs. Low had found:

When Two People Are at One
I Ching (9th century BC)

When two people are at one
in their inmost hearts
They shatter even the strength of iron
or of bronze
And when two people understand each other
in their inmost hearts
Their words are sweet and strong
like the fragrance of orchids.

Mr. Low led everyone out of the room and into the restaurant where the guests now sat at the round tables.

Unlike the banquet disaster, this festive meal was one of great joy. Hop Sun's smile was wider than ever, his eyes shining with happiness. Li too, was smiling. Two men carried the sofa with Mrs. Low on it into the restaurant so she could take part.

"If we were rich, I'd hire these two men for the next three months," Mrs. Low said happily.

"They could carry me around town. I would be quite the sight."

Mr. Low served fish – a symbol for abundance – as the main course. Ty looked around that table and beamed. In fact, his face hurt from all the smiling. These were his friends, he thought: Mrs. Doyle, Eva, Mr. and Mrs. Low, Li and Hop Sun. Oh, and of course, Minus. They all were Ty's friends, and in a way, his family.

As they were eating the last course, the door of the restaurant opened and a middle-aged man wearing a black bowler hat and a suit walked in. Everyone stopped eating and looked at him. Eva gasped.

"Father!" she said and ran to the man's open arms.

***

Later, after all of the excitement of Dr. Doyle being reunited with his wife and daughter as well as the final festivities of Hop Sun and Li's wedding, Eva pulled Ty aside.

"Father told me as soon as he got my letter, he went to a special hospital for help. He said it was so hard...he wanted to die...but he had a photograph of Mother and me, and he kept saying he would see us again. After the treatment, he took the train out here."

Fear twisted Ty's stomach. "What will you do?" he asked, not wanting to know the answer.

Eva looked at him gravely. "We will return to New York. That's where Father's practice is. And our house."

Ty's stomach dropped. It was true. They would leave. All the joy was sucked out of the day.

***

That night as he lay in his bed in the barn, he felt a heavy sadness. He should have been happy, he knew, because his best friend's father had come back to her, cured. But his friend was leaving. He scratched Minus's head, and the sleeping dog kept snoring lightly. Angel was stretched out at the end of his blanket, and Ty couldn't help but noticed how shiny his fur was now. He was a healthy-looking cat, although every bit as ornery. Ty reached out to pet him three times and then withdrew his hand before Angel could bite him. Ty loved that cat, irritable temperament, and all. His dog and his cat were his friends. They wouldn't leave him.

***

After their wedding, Li and Hop Sun worked very hard at the laundry. They woke at 5:30 in the morning and toiled all day. Hop Sun, sweat pouring down his face, bent over the tubs of boiling water, stirring the clothes. Li helped the best she could with her one good arm.

The work was hard and long. Still, it enabled them to buy rice and vegetables. They could survive. They could walk outside on a clear day and look up; if they were lucky they would see the majestic Mount Rainier and their spirits would revive.

Mrs. Low found another Chinese poem for Li. "This is like Mount Rainier," she said.

In the Country
Li Yu (937-978)

My neighbor runs to me with
The news, "look out your window!"
For days the mountain was
Invisible. This morning
It shines bright and new
As though it had been washed.

CHAPTER 22: WRECKING THE RALLY

A fish not caught by a hook
may be caught by a net.
(Vary your strategies.)

It was now the end of October. Eva's parents had decided to go back to New York at the end of November after Mrs. Doyle had fulfilled her business obligations. In the meantime, Dr. Doyle helped out whenever another doctor needed an extra hand or a second opinion. "I will not be performing surgery," he told his wife. "I dare not be around drugs that reduce pain." Eva often heard her parents talking in low voices late into the night. They had much to talk over, and sometimes she could hear her mother cry. Perhaps it was a happy cry.

Every day Dr. Doyle checked on Mrs. Low to make sure she and her baby were still doing well.

"You give me great comfort," Mrs. Low told him. "For a few minutes, at least, I can send worry to fly out the window. Usually worry flies back in, but soon...soon, our wait will be over."

"Let's keep worry out of our minds," said Dr. Doyle. "I challenge you to a game of chess." Dr.

Doyle was a good chess player and relished challenging Mrs. Low and Ty. With two opponents now to practice with, Ty was rapidly improving. He often beat Mrs. Low now.

"I can't think clearly on this sofa," Mrs. Low complained. "I blame everything on this sofa. The blood doesn't circulate as well to my head when I'm reclining. When I can sit upright, after this baby is born, you will never win."

Ty laughed. Then Eva came in holding a poster. "Look at this," she said angrily and proceeded to read it: "The Chinese Must Go! Mayor Weisbach has called a MASS MEETING for this (Saturday) evening at 7:30 o'clock AT ALPHA OPERA HOUSE to consider the Chinese question. TURN OUT."

Eva scowled. "Mayor Weisbach and his cronies need their comeuppance," she said.

She took out a pencil and wrote a "B" over the "T" on the poster, so it instead of "Turn Out" it said "Burn Out."

Ty looked at her questioningly. Eva looked back at him and her angry expression changed. Her eyes had a special glint that meant she was thinking of a plan.

"We can't stop the rally or the group from Seattle from coming," she said. "But we can be the fly in the ointment."

Ty had no idea what that meant. Why were people always talking about flies? Ty tried to imagine a fly in ointment and ended up feeling sorry for the stuck bug.

"It means we will keep the rally from going smoothly," Eva explained. "If we can bring just a little unhappiness to the celebration, a little chaos or mess-up, I'd say we'd have contributed to a good cause."

Ty was always willing to help, whatever Eva wanted to do. And so Eva started planning.

***

Mayor Weisbach was looking forward to the big anti-Chinese mass meeting to be held in Tacoma on November 2, just a few days away. Seattle's anti-Chinese group was coming, and he would show them a thing or two. If this event was successful, they'd see just what a skilled leader he was. All of Tacoma would be impressed too. The thought of running for governor flitted through his brain more frequently these days. Soon, thanks in part to his efforts, the Chinese would be gone from Tacoma. The town would be

tidy again. This meeting would rally his supporters and win new ones. For now, he just had to
make sure that posters were distributed all over
town.

***

At recess the next day, Eva called together Ty
and the girls in her class who now adamantly
supported the Chinese. They spent that recess
and a couple hours after school thinking of some
"fun" or ways to bring chaos to the meeting. Eva
was an extremely clever girl, Ty thought later,
and he was very glad she was on his side, not
against him.

On the evening of the rally, Mayor Weisbach
and a few of his cronies went to the train station
to meet the contingent from Seattle. He was surprised to see that none of his supporters were
there. "Where is everyone?" he asked. "I told the
band to be here! We need music to welcome Seattle. We need people to cheer. We want to show
them Tacoma's spirit."

Then a man ran up to him. "Mayor! There you
are! Why aren't you down at the dock? The people from Seattle are arriving any second."

"Why the dock? They are coming by train!"
sputtered Mayor Weisbach.

"But we got an official letter saying the Seattle group had changed their transportation from train to boat, so the band went to the dock," the man said, confused.

"I gave no such notice," Mayor Weisbach said. "The band is supposed to be <u>here</u>. We're supposed to have a glorious welcome. Now it will be pathetic."

He could do nothing except send the man back to the docks to tell the band and all others to head to the Alpha Opera House where the speeches would be held. When the train pulled in, only Mayor Weisbach and three of his men welcomed the Seattle group. This was not starting out well. At least he knew he had a good speech written, guaranteed to stir everyone up. Even though he was seething inside, he put on a jovial face and led the Seattle group to the Opera House. Mayor Weisbach did not like it when things didn't go as planned.

**

At the hall, people were disappointed because they'd gone to the wrong meeting spot. It was dark now, and they ran to the wagon that held the signs, grabbed them, and hurried to assemble for the torchlight march.

The mayor and the Seattle group arrived just then and were surprised to see signs that said "The Chinese Must Stay." And "Chinese. Yes, yes, yes!" When the sign-holders looked at what they were waving, they angrily tossed the signs away.

Meanwhile, people couldn't get their torches lit. Cloth had been wrapped around one end of long sticks, but the cloth had been soaked in water. The torches couldn't be ignited. Mayor Weisbach was furious.

A large cannon was sounded to announce the festivities. But someone had untied all of the horses, and when the horses heard the boom, they panicked and ran. Some of the men left to try to find them, reducing the number of people in the march. "We have been sabotaged!" Mayor Weisbach cried. But there was nothing to be done.

Men and women were already filing into the Opera House, ready for a show. Mayor Weisbach had elicited the promise of many anti-Chinese women to sit in the front row of the balcony and wave their scarves in support of his speech. But Eva and her friends got there first. Mayor Weisbach's group had to sit, hidden behind Eva's loud and boisterous group.

The brass band on stage started to play patriotic music. People in the audience excitedly chattered to one another. When the band started playing "My Country 'Tis of Thee" everyone stood up to sing:

My country, 'tis of thee,
Sweet land of liberty,
Of thee I sing;
Land where my fathers died,
Land of the pilgrims' pride,
From every mountainside
Let freedom ring!

Mayor Weisbach had pre-set his speech on the podium in the middle of the stage. He walked to the podium, smiling and waving at the audience. Eva's group made loud raspberry sounds, catcalls and boos as he walked.

Rattled, he picked up his speech. He looked at the paper to begin to read and stopped. Someone had replaced his speech with a grocery list. His face turned red. He was in front of all these people and what was he to say? He certainly wasn't going to say "One dozen eggs, a quart of milk, a pound of beef." He looked out at the audience. Everyone looked expectantly up at him, waiting for his words of wisdom. "Think, Weisbach!" he told himself. Eventually he found words, but they weren't half as glorious as the ones he had written. He forgot several key points. But he rallied near the end when he raised his hands and cried out, "It is time! The Chinese will go! We have devised a plan to expel the Chinese completely from Tacoma."

He leaned forward on the podium. "We have appointed a Committee of Fifteen. They have organized and soon will carry out our plan. But we will need all of you! Be prepared to heed the call. Be prepared!" The audience buzzed with excitement. What did he mean?

Mayor Weisbach remembered his ending line. He shook his finger at the crowd and said, "When the laws fail to protect the people, the people are duty bound to protect themselves!" Everyone cheered. Mayor Weisbach smiled, pleased with himself for pulling it together at the end.

But he had one more unfortunate surprise. The big celebration party afterwards was to feature the huge cake lovingly made by old Mrs. Budlow. It was the prettiest cake anyone had ever seen with candied flowers and the words "Chinese Must Go!" written in pink icing. At least this cake will provide a fitting ending,

Mayor Weisbach thought. Mrs. Budlow's cakes were famous far and wide.

The enormous cake was rolled out on stage. Mrs. Budlow walked behind it, beaming.

"We will serve Mrs. Budlow's famous cake in the lobby after we are dismissed here," announced Mayor Weisbach proudly. "Mrs. Budlow, would you do the honor of cutting this?"

Still beaming but trying to appear modest, Mrs. Budlow cut a big piece of cake and handed it to the mayor.

He took one bite and...spit it out! Horrible! The luscious white frosting tasted like soap! Mayor Weisbach turned to look with horror at Mrs. Budlow. What had she done? Was she trying to poison him?

The audience was surprised to see their mayor spitting out the anticipated dessert. What was going on?

Mrs. Budlow tasted it, spit it out too, and started sobbing. "I don't know what happened. I just don't know. Oh my reputation is ruined!" The people in the audience started to talk among themselves.

Mayor Weisbach had to shout to be heard. "No cake! Go home everyone!" he yelled. From the balcony, Eva's friends cheered and happily waved their kerchiefs.

Flustered, Mayor Weisbach signaled for the band to play. The audience, disappointed not to get cake, grumbled and filed out. The Seattle anti-Chinese group headed home, secretly pleased that Tacoma's rally was a flop. Seattle could do it better, naturally.

"Come to Seattle next time," the leader of the Seattle group said to Mayor Weisbach as they left. "We'll show you how to plan a good rally."

Mayor Weisbach went to bed that night tired, irritated, and very unhappy. Maybe politics weren't in his future. It was too chancy. People were much too fickle.

On the other hand, Eva told Ty that night that she was considering a future in organizing people and events. "Maybe I'll run for mayor when I'm old enough," she said. "I could show these people a thing or two."

Ty agreed.

CHAPTER 23: THE WORST DAY
In deep water and fierce fire
(A day of great trouble)

The weather was so raw and cold in early November that Ty had finally been forced to leave the barn and go back to sleeping inside by the kitchen stove. Every night he locked Minus and Angel in the barn to keep them safe. He hated to be apart from them at night, but the barn was just too cold.

It was hard being indoors because he couldn't avoid his pa and his brothers. Mostly they left him alone, but sometimes they'd be bored and start teasing him. Occasionally Pa would be drunk and try to wallop him. Ty was quick and mostly avoided any blows, but he always had to be on his guard. He never knew what to expect from his pa or his brothers.

***

Before he even opened his eyes the morning of November 3, Ty knew something was wrong. He could hear his pa and brothers up, moving around, getting dressed. It was too early for them to be awake. What was going on? Then his pa and brothers came into the kitchen. Sam grabbed Ty by his shirt. "Get some wood," he said, dragging him out of his blanket.

Ty pulled on his boots and coat and stumbled out the front door into the dark, into the rain, to grab firewood from the covered area by the porch. Why were they up? Ty brought in the wood, put two pieces in the stove and retreated to his corner, willing himself to be invisible.

Nobody was interested in him. Instead, they talked in low, excited voices as they made and then gulped down hot coffee. "Today we'll get rid of the Chinese," Pa said, almost gleefully. "This is gonna be fun."

Ty couldn't believe what he'd heard. They were going to get rid of the Chinese? His insides started to get shaky.

His pa and brothers put on their coats and hats and left. Ty watched to see the direction they headed, then he waited a few minutes, grabbed his own coat and cap, and went to the barn to let Minus and Angel out. As a second thought, he took out the two twenty-dollar bills from the trunk and tucked them into his pocket. He had a feeling they might come in handy.

Ty, with Minus at his side, set off down the hill. It was still dark. The rain was penetrating and cold. He could see flickering torches down on

236

Pacific. Something was happening. Lots of people were heading down the hill too. Something must have been arranged the night before.

When Ty reached Pacific, he saw groups of men moving down the street. Ty ran down the boardwalk to the restaurant. He could see the lights were on there. The door was unlocked. Ty tentatively pushed the door open and entered. Mr. Low came out from the back office, in great agitation.

"Ty! The baby is coming," Mr. Low said. "We came here an hour ago because we heard a commotion and we wanted to protect the store. But now Mrs. Low is having the baby. The time is here. There is no stopping it now. Of all the times, why today?"

Mr. Low looked anguished. "I fear she will die in childbirth. Listen! She is in pain! She screams. Mrs. Low is never in pain, she is always in control! Please, what can we do? Why today? I need to get a doctor, but I can't leave her side."

"I'll go," said Ty. From the office, he could hear Mrs. Low calling out in Chinese. Then she screamed in pain.

"Hurry," said Mr. Low, his voice cracking. "Please, run. Please get Dr. Doyle."

"I will," said Ty, immediately turning around and leaving. Shaken at seeing Mr. Low's panic, he ran as fast as he could to the Doyles' house. He pounded frantically on the door. Minus, of course, had come with him and sat by the front door expectantly, knowing he'd get food at this house. In a minute, Mrs. Doyle, wearing a wrap over her nightgown and looking sleepy, answered. "Ty!" she said, surprised to see him at that early hour.

"The baby is coming," he said, panting. "Mrs. Low needs help. Dr. Doyle needs to come. But something bad is happening. Men with guns are down there. Pa said they're gonna get rid of the Chinese. Hurry."

"Oh dear," said Mrs. Doyle. "The baby. We must help them. I'll get Dr. Doyle." By this time, Eva had heard the noise and had come to the door, standing behind her mother.

"I'm coming too," she said. "Ty, eat something while we get ready." She and Mrs. Doyle went to change clothes, and even though Ty wasn't hungry for once in his life, he chewed on a piece of bread, giving Minus half.

When Dr. Doyle had dressed and grabbed his bag, all four of them plus Minus ran through the rain back to the restaurant.

Ty led the doctor to the office and opened the door. Mrs. Doyle followed her husband into the room, but Ty didn't even want to look in. The idea of Mrs. Low in pain and laboring to give birth frightened him. He, Eva, and Minus stayed out in the restaurant, sitting at one of the dining tables and trying not to listen to Mrs. Low's cries. The sounds agitated Minus. He whined and kept running to the office door.

Suddenly, they heard people shouting outside the restaurant. Ty got up and peered out the window. He saw men running through the rain, carrying rifles, big sticks and torches.

Would these men make Mrs. Low leave? Going out in the rain and traveling in a wagon would be horrible for her. It could kill her. What if she or the baby died? Ty couldn't bear to think those thoughts. He sat down at one of the tables and tried to do math problems in his head, to keep from thinking bad thoughts. Eva looked as if she was praying. Minus kept whining and running to the front door, to the office, and then back to Ty.

A short time later, Dr. Doyle and Mr. Low came out to get more hot water and clean towels. "We can only wait now for nature and Mrs. Low to bring forth this child," Dr. Doyle told them.

Mr. Low leaned weakly on a chair. "Oh doctor, if there is anything you can do...so they both can live...if only they both will live, I would have nothing more to ask for in this life."

"I will do the best I can. It's not up to me," Dr. Doyle said, and motioned Mr. Low to come with him back to the office.

From outside Ty could hear more shouting. "Over here! Almost time to start!" a man yelled.

Just then, a whistle blasted in the distance. "WOOOOOO!"

"It's from Lister's Foundry," Eva said. "That must be the signal."

"Wooo! Wooooo!" More work whistles.

"Several businesses must be in on this plan," she said.

What was going to happen? There was nothing to do but wait. Wait for the baby and wait for the angry mob. It was like waiting for a storm to hit. Ty nervously walked around Mr. Low's restaurant. Minus followed him anxiously.

"Why don't you go down the street and see what's happening?" said Eva.

Ty nodded, pulled on his coat and cap and stepped outside. The rain was falling harder now. Down the street he could see a large group of men waving pistols and big sticks. The wind made the rain colder. Everything was dark gray – the sky, the rain, the muddy street, the buildings. Ty headed towards the mob.

At each Chinese store, Ty saw a few armed men leave the group and pound on the door. When the door opened, the men pushed their way inside. Some dragged out a struggling Chinese worker. Others shouted at the Chinese people inside, "Get out! All Chinese must get out of Tacoma! No more Chinese here! Get out!"

Hundreds of excited men filled the street. Some headed up the side streets.

"Chinese! Out!" the ones in the front yelled. The men behind them chanted, "The Chinese must go! The Chinese must go!"

As Ty got near to Ah Wing's laundry, he wondered if Li and Hop Sun were in there. Half a block away from the laundry, he saw a man pound on the door. Ah Wing opened it and two men grabbed him. "But I cannot leave my business!" Ah Wing cried. "I have customers' clothes still in my tubs! I have to return their clothes!"

"You didn't believe us, did you?" one tall skinny man said, waving a rifle. "You didn't think we'd really make you leave! You was wrong! Get out!" The two men dragged Ah Wing out into the street and threw him into a wagon pulled by a sad-looking horse.

Ah Wing struggled to sit up. "I wired the governor!" he shouted to anyone within earshot. "I said 'Mob driving Chinamen out of town. Will you not protect us?' And the governor did not answer! We have been abandoned! This country has turned its back on us!"

Then Ty saw men pulling Li and Hop Sun out of the building.

"Don't hurt her arm," Hop Sun pleaded with the men. "It is not yet healed. We will come with you peacefully."

The men prodded them with a rifle and Li, furious, turned to them. "<u>Do</u> <u>not</u> <u>touch</u> <u>me</u>," she said. Her fierceness must have scared the men because they stepped back. Hop Sun and Li walked over to the wagon and climbed in with as much dignity as they could. The wind was now blowing the rain at a slant.

Ty ran to them. "Hop Sun! Li!" He waved his arms at them frantically.

Hop Sun turned to look. Ty had never seen such an expression on his friend's face. It was a look of confusion mixed with shame. Li's expression was angry and defiant. More than anything, Ty wanted to save his friends, to protect them from these bullies, but he was just a boy, power-less to help. The helpless feeling that he knew so well overwhelmed him and he wanted to cry. Instead, he just stood there, looking up at his friends in total misery.

"Don't worry," said Li, seeing the anguish on his face. "Hop Sun always says things will work out. This is putting his beliefs to the test." Hop Sun actually smiled at that.

The rain continued driving down steady and hard. The wagon carrying Hop Sun and Li creaked as it started to move off. Li lifted her hand to wave farewell. Ty watched them until the wagon turned a corner to go up the hill, and then he slowly walked back to the restaurant.

There, Mr. Low was with Eva, pacing, distressed. From the office they could hear more cries, screams, and string of Chinese words from Mrs. Low.

"Why won't the baby come" Mr. Low asked them, although he didn't really seem to expect them to answer. "What is wrong? Something is wrong. I will lose my wife, my baby, my home, my business. I will lose everything."

Outside, the angry voices were getting closer. Mr. Low went to the window, looked out, and then came back.

"I came to America fifteen years ago, and Tacoma ten years ago," Mr. Low said in agitation. "This is my home. My business. Yet these men are driving me out. This is America! There are laws."

Ty didn't like to see Mr. Low so upset. He'd always been calm, now he was practically in tears. Weren't grown-ups in control? If they couldn't handle things, how could he?

Ty started to get that familiar hopeless feeling again but then he got a sudden thought: this was like a chess game, wasn't it, one side pitted against another. Two can play the game. He tried to quiet his mind and see the "board." This game was being played in Tacoma, on Pacific Avenue, in this restaurant and back room where Mrs. Low was laboring. In chess, Ty knew what he had to do to win. So did his opponent. In this situation, Ty realized the "players" might be using different rules, with different goals. For Mayor Weisbach and his gang, a win today would mean removing all of the Chinese. They were attempting that by brute force.

Ty's goal was different. He would win if he helped Mrs. Low and the baby live, and keep their family together. He had to achieve that by careful strategy. The pieces for his side were right before him: Mr. Low, Mrs. Low, Hop Sun, Li, Mrs. Doyle, Eva, Mr. Doyle and himself. Minus too.

As in chess, Ty knew he might have to sacrifice some of his pieces in order to win. Thinking clearly, he could see that Hop Sun and Li may have to leave Tacoma. He hated to see them go but they could survive wherever they ended up. Perhaps, though, they could help the Low family by leaving a smoke screen as they left. The next move? Eva could act as a decoy. Mrs. Doyle and Dr. Doyle would have to protect the queen, in this case Mrs. Low. Mr. Low, the King, could distract the enemy in order to save the Queen.

Yes, Ty could see the game now. His mind was focused. Time to play. Here was his plan: Eva could pretend to be Mrs. Low. She could be wrapped in a blanket and moan like a laboring woman until they got to the yard where the Chinese were being held. The real Mrs. Low could continue to labor at the restaurant, and when she gave birth and it was safe, she could reunite with Mr. Low. Dr. Doyle and Mrs. Doyle could take them to Seattle. The Chinese situation in Seattle hadn't yet reached Tacoma's dismal low.

Ty told Mrs. Doyle his plan, and Mrs. Doyle quietly relayed it to Mr. Low.

"If the mob comes here and wants to take you and your wife, you will have to go," she told him. "Eva can play the part of Mrs. Low. The real Mrs. Low will be here, so she can have the baby in safety."

"I can't leave my wife now," said Mr. Low. "Please, I must stay."

"It'll only be for a short time," said Mrs. Doyle. "You will meet back up tonight. Mrs. Low can't be moved until after the baby is born. You know that, don't you? Think of the lifetime you will have with Mrs. Low and the baby. We have the best doctor in the Territory here in Dr. Doyle. This is our only hope. But you must go. Please."

Mr. Low closed his eyes for a second. Then he opened them and said, "I will go. I know she will be in good hands. My heart will be here, even if my body will be elsewhere."

And when the bullies came knocking on the restaurant door, Mr. Low was there to open it.

"Get out. Get in the wagons. We told you to leave and by God, now you will," said one of the men.

"Please. My wife is going to have a baby," said Mr. Low.

The men laughed. "Go get her or else we'll drag her out." Mr. Low went into the office and

246

in a few minutes came out with Eva wrapped in a blanket, pretending to be Mrs. Low. Eva was so vocal as a woman in labor though, that Mrs. Doyle had to whisper to her, "Be quiet! Don't attract any more attention than you have to."

Mr. Low carried "Mrs. Low" into the wagon, as the rain pelted down at them. The driver was so wet, irritable, and afraid that this pregnant woman would give birth in his wagon that he decided to take them to the meeting place at once, not bothering to pick up any more Chinese. He just wanted to unload them and get home to his dry warm house.

Once the wagon jostled away, Ty stuffed Dr. Doyle's coat and hat into the doctor's satchel. Then he and Minus ran up the hill heading to the yard where the Chinese were being brought. As he ran, he felt a knot of fear in his stomach. Would this work? What if it didn't? What if they discovered Mrs. Low at the restaurant and made her leave? It'd be all Ty's fault for thinking up this plan. Then he remembered one of Mrs. Low's proverbs: "The man who says it can't be done should not interrupt the person doing it." He just needed to do it. He had to try. Ty bent his head to protect his face from the driving rain and tried to run faster up the hill. Minus was right by his side, eager to race his beloved master. What was rain to him?

Fifteen minutes later, they arrived at the courtyard which was now filled with distraught Chinese men, women and children. The wagon with Mr. Low and Eva had just arrived. Mr. Low carried "Mrs. Low" out of the wagon, to wait with the other Chinese people in the holding area. The white man who was trying to keep track of the Chinese people saw them and started to walk over to get their names written down.

Ty saw this and made a quick decision. "Run, Minus. Let's have fun. Go, dog," Ty said, chasing after him and clapping his hands when he got close. Minus loved this game and ran around crazily, barking and weaving through people, splashing through puddles. Ty pursued his dog, yelling as he went. The white man coming towards them stopped. He'd never seen a three-legged dog before. How did that dog balance? By the time the man turned back to his duties, Mr. Low and "Mrs. Low" had blended into a large group of Chinese men. The white man wasn't sure where the new arrivals had gone. He shrugged. What difference did it make? They'd all be gone soon. He turned back to meet a new wagon filled with more unhappy Chinese people.

The people in the waiting area were so busy watching as the boy chased his three-legged dog that no one noticed when "Mrs. Low" slipped out of the blanket and became Eva again. Nobody was keeping track of anything now. Women were crying. The few children present were wailing, clinging to their mothers' hands. Everyone was cold, wet, and miserable. Rain kept falling. Li and Hop Sun who had arrived earlier saw Mr. Low and came over to him. They, Eva, and Ty surrounded Mr. Low, and Ty handed him Dr. Doyle's overcoat and slightly crushed bowler hat. Mr. Low put on the coat, turned the collar of the coat up and pulled the bowler hat down low so that he looked much like the other white men, milling about. The three of them, Eva, Ty and "Dr. Doyle" walked away. Hop Sun and Li quietly watched them go. They couldn't say wave or say farewell. They could only watch and hope for the best as their friends headed back down to the restaurant.

Ty briefly wondered if he'd ever see Hop Sun and Li again. Then he got an idea. He turned around and ran back to them. "Here," he said, thrusting the twenty-dollar bills into Li's hand. "I found this in my ma's trunk. You may need it."

And before Li could even thank him, he turned around and caught up with Eva and Mr. Low.

Now he had to put Li and Hop Sun out of his mind and think of the next move. The "chess game" was still in progress. They hurried down the hill to the back door of the restaurant and snuck inside. As they took off their coats, they heard a strange noise coming from the office. A cry. A cry of a baby! It had been born! The baby had been born!

Mr. Low ran into the back room. Ty and Eva kept guard at the doors, hoping no one from the mobs would be coming around, double-checking on who was in the store. No one should be checking because everyone had seen Mr. Low and Mrs. Low leave in the wagon, but who could predict what those bullies would do? Minus sensed something was going on in the office and stood eagerly at the door, whining to get in.

Mrs. Doyle came out then, her eyes shining, her smile broad. "It's a girl," she said to Eva and Ty. "Come see."

Eva ran into the room, but Ty was shy. He peeked in at the door and saw Mrs. Low sitting up in bed, holding a little bundle wrapped in a blanket. Mr. Low was sitting on a chair, looking overwhelmed and stunned. Dr. Doyle stood by, looking at them proudly.

"Healthy baby girl," he said. "Mother and daughter are fighters."

Just then they heard noise from the front of the restaurant. Someone was coming in the front door. Mrs. Doyle pulled Ty into the office and rushed out while Eva quickly locked the office door behind her.

"Get out, lady," they heard a man's rough voice say. "You don't belong here."

Mrs. Doyle said, "This is my restaurant now. I bought it."

They could hear the man's voice say, "Lady, this is a Chinese place, and we aim to burn it to the ground."

"Over my dead body," said Mrs. Doyle, her voice rising. "I bought it fair and square. I have the deed right here. I got a great deal on it from the owner who had to sell it fast."

She must have produced the deed because he said, "All right then, but you should still get out of here. Chinese buildings may be set on fire soon. I can't guarantee this won't be burned too. We aim to remove every trace of the Chinese."

The door closed, and Mrs. Doyle returned to the office, her eyes worried. "We must hurry," she said. "It isn't safe here. Dr. Doyle and I will go to the stables and hire Jeb Hanks to take the Lows to Seattle. Jeb is honest. It's a good thing Dr. Doyle brought his wallet with him."

Dr. Doyle chuckled, and he and his wife went off to arrange for the wagon. Eva and Ty watched Mr. and Mrs. Low crying, laughing, and kissing the baby. At least Ty assumed there was a baby there. It was wrapped in a blanket and covered up by Mr. and Mrs. Low bending over it. There couldn't be a happier moment even in the middle of all of the chaos, fear, and injustice around them.

Mrs. Low looked up and beckoned Eva and Ty to come over. "Ty, look!"

Ty cautiously crept over to her and was amazed at the little red baby face peering out from the blanket. He'd never seen a newborn up close. The little girl had lots of black hair and a red, scrunched up face. Ty hoped the baby was all right. Did all babies look so scrunched up right after being born? He looked up to see tears streaming down the face of Mrs. Low.

"The proverb says 'There is only one perfect child, and every mother thinks her child is it," she said "In this case, it is true. I have the perfect child."

"Are you going to chop up the couch now?" Ty asked, remembering Mrs. Low's comment from months before.

She kissed her baby and laughed. "No, this is my lucky couch. If we didn't have to leave now, I'd make a shrine out of it." She kissed her baby five more times.

A little while later they heard a wagon come up the back alley. Mrs. Doyle came in the back door. "Come now," she said. "Hurry."

Mr. Low walked to the center of his restaurant and looked around. "This was mine," he said bitterly. "They have forced me out. I built this all from nothing. And I must do it again somewhere else."

Then he quickly put on Dr. Doyle's coat and hat again and carried his wife and baby to the wagon. Dr. and Mrs. Doyle planned to accompany them to the boat.

"Good luck," said Eva, and she and Ty followed them outside. "God speed."

After they climbed into the wagon, Mrs. Low kissed her baby three more times and looked up at her friends. "A long journey starts with a single step," she said. "We begin our journey now. We will miss you."

"And we'll miss you," said Eva. "Write us when you can."

Mr. Low, tears running down his face, lifted his hand in a wave of farewell.

Jeb Hanks snapped the reins, and soon the wagon was out of sight. Eva and Ty turned around and went back into the office. They were tidying it up when they heard a noise out in the restaurant. They ran out and saw the door to the restaurant fly open. Ty's pa and two brothers burst in. Ty recognized the crazed fury on his pa's face. He'd already been drinking, at this hour? Ty's insides started getting shaky.

"Sam saw you come in here," growled Pa, his teeth clenched, his eyes bloodshot. "What did I tell you? You get the hell out of this Chinese dump." In two long strides, he was over to Ty and walloped him alongside the head. Ty went sprawling. Minus ran over to him, agitated.

"Stop that!" cried, Eva, stepping up to help. Ty's pa whirled.

"Shut up," he snarled, and he lifted his hand and hit her too. She fell to the floor. She'd never been hit by anyone before, especially a grown man. She was stunned and just laid there, trying to collect her wits. Ty scrambled to his feet and stood in front of her.

"If you hit her again, I'll..." Ty didn't know what he'd do, but he just couldn't allow Eva to be hit. His pa lunged at him and pulled him up off his feet. Ty could smell his foul breath and the body odor on his dirty clothes. Pa raised his arm to hit him.

Then Ty heard something. A low growl. Minus. The dog wasn't going to let anybody hurt his beloved master and friend. Snarling, he leapt at Pa, sinking his teeth into Pa's leg. His pants tore, and blood started seeping out.

"Get that damn dog off me!" Pa yelled, trying to push at the angry dog. But Minus held on, growling and furious. Off balanced, Pa took out his gun.

"No!" screamed Eva from her spot on the ground. Ty reached up to push the gun away, but Pa shot. The sound was loud and violent. Minus jerked and fell to the ground.

Ty's pa stepped over the dog and grabbed Ty by the coat. "Boys, take this sonofabitch home and lock him in my room," Pa said. "I'll deal with him after we clear out the Chinese." He thrust Ty into the hands of his brothers who dragged him out of the restaurant into the driving rain. Pa left to join other men down the street who were marching and shouting. Sam and Fred

255

started hauling the sobbing Ty up the hill to their house.

The wind still slapped the cold rain at Ty's face as his brother pushed and shoved him.

Tears ran down his face. "Please, let me go. Let me go back," he begged. "I gotta help my dog. Please."

Sam shook his head and growled, "That mutt is dead. Pa shot him in the heart."

"No!" cried Ty.

Ty struggled to look at Fred. Fred was once his friend. Maybe he still was.

"Fred, please?"

Fred wouldn't look at him. "Just keep moving," Fred mumbled. "Won't do you no good to go back. Your dog is dead. I'm sorry, Ty."

Ty wouldn't believe it. It wasn't true. His dog couldn't be dead.

"Let me go!" cried Ty, but Sam ignored him.

The chill cut through Ty's soggy coat. His teeth chattered and his body shivered, and he couldn't make them stop. The hike up the hill to their house had never taken so long.

When they got home, Sam dragged Ty to Pa's room, shoved him in, closed the door and propped a chair under the doorknob on the other side to lock him in.

Ty looked wildly around the room for an escape. The bedroom window had long ago been boarded up when the glass broke and Pa didn't want to replace it. Ty couldn't get out that way. He tried the door again, but it wouldn't budge.

Ty looked out the keyhole and saw his brothers sitting at the kitchen table, talking about the Chinese. Sam bragged about how many he'd dragged out of the buildings.

Drenched, cold, and shivering, Ty sat on Pa's filthy bed. He took off his wet clothes, wrapped himself up in a blanket, and sat on the edge of the bed, sobbing. After a while, he heard his pa stagger into the house. He looked through the keyhole and saw his pa had brought home whiskey. Pa and his brothers drank and talked, "Them Chinese were so scared, weren't they?" crowed Pa. "We're gonna get great jobs now. Wait and see."

Heartbroken, Ty curled up on the floor by the door and lay there, thinking of poor Minus and all the things he'd learned since he'd first gotten the dog. Minus had changed his life. Ty had met Eva because of the dog. Ty learned to read a little. He learned to eat properly. He learned he wasn't stupid, that was a big thing. And he learned about love. He knew Minus loved him, and he loved Minus. He remembered the dog's big brown eyes and how they looked at him as if he was the greatest person in the whole wide world. Ty started sobbing and cried until he was too exhausted to stay awake.

CHAPTER 24: THE NEXT DAY

One happiness scatters a thousand sorrows.

Ty woke up early the next morning, and the memory of what happened the day before flooded back into his memory. Minus. Mrs. Low. The baby. Hop Sun and Li. He jumped up, pulled on his clothes, and tried the door. Someone – probably Fred – had moved the chair from the other side of the door. Ty cautiously opened it. His pa was sleeping at the kitchen table, his rifle across his knees, his head back, snoring. Sam had his head down on the table. Empty bottles surrounded them. Fred most likely was up in attic, sleeping.

Ty quietly walked past Pa and Sam to the front door. He knew what he had to do. First, he ran to the barn. He hadn't had time to lock Angel in last night, so the cat had found a mostly dry place to sleep in the covered woodpile. Ty flung open the barn door and Angel ran over to him, irritated at having to spend the night outside but hoping today was a day he'd get some food.

Ty stood at the door and looked at the barn's interior. Despair and hopelessness filled every inch of his being. He'd lost everything. He

259

couldn't live with his pa and brothers anymore. He knew that. So, he lost his home. He lost his Chinese friends, and he was soon to lose Eva and Mrs. Doyle when they moved. His dog was dead. He had nothing.

Well, that wasn't true. He looked down at the cat, his ornery cat. Angel rubbed against Ty's legs, looking up expectantly at his master. The cat needed Ty, and Ty needed the cat.

Ty went to the trunk, opened it and took out the photo of his ma, the box with the letters, and the old Bible. He put them in a burlap bag and slung it over his shoulder. Then with the towel that served as Angel's bed, he picked up the cat, wrapped the animal securely so he couldn't scratch, and left the barn.

The cat was heavy and squirming, but Ty would not loosen his grip. He'd go to the Doyles' house, that's what he'd do. They could help him figure out where to go and what to do next.

As he walked down the hill, he tried to come up with a plan. He could work odd jobs at a restaurant, then he'd always have food. Maybe he could sleep in the restaurant's kitchen and Angel could keep it free of rodents. He and Angel would be a team.

The sky was gray, and the weather was cold and raw but not raining. Ty shivered. His coat was still damp from yesterday. Angel stopped squirming, perhaps saving his strength for a big escape effort later. Ty missed having Minus running next to him. His heart ached.

He had to find out what had happened to Mr. and Mrs. Low and their baby. Did they make it to the boat for Seattle? Where were Hop Sun and Li? Where was his dog's body?

When he reached Pacific, he saw people clumped in little groups on the boardwalk. As he got closer, he heard one man waving the morning newspaper. "Good riddance to 'em," the man said. "Look at them headlines. 'GONE! 200 Chinese Gone! How the People's Will was Enacted.'"

Ty's stomach ached from hunger. He hadn't eaten since yesterday morning at Eva's house. He was famished but felt too miserable to eat. He could bear anything, if only Minus was by his side. Well, Minus wasn't at his side. Minus was dead. Today Ty would bury Minus. He'd take his dog into the woods, to the clearing where sunlight streamed through the trees, and he would dig a grave. And if Ty stayed in Tacoma, he'd go there often, to be with Minus.

He felt a sob start to come up his throat, but he shook his head. He had to be tougher. He had started to get soft, and when you're soft, you get hurt. Ty felt his stomach growl again. He hurried on to Mr. Low's restaurant.

The door was opened. He stepped into the restaurant and stopped. He immediately looked to where Minus had been shot. Dried blood remained on the floor. A couple of chairs were still overturned on the ground where Ty's pa had knocked them over in his rage. Ty closed the door behind him and set Angel on the floor. The cat glared at him.

Where had Eva taken Minus? Ty didn't know what to do or where to go. He dropped to his knees, helpless and hopeless.

Just then the office door opened. Mrs. Doyle stood there for a second looking at the grieving boy. She went over to him and put her arm around him.

"Come here," she said and led him into the back office.

Ty's heart started beating fast. Was Minus there? He wasn't sure he could stand to see that little body. But he knew he must. He owed it to his Minus.

The room was dark when he stepped in. The curtains were closed, and it was hard for Ty to make out what was there. Eva sat in the chair. Dr. Doyle stood by her. On the couch where Mrs. Low usually lay was Minus.

A sob came up in Ty's throat.

The little dog was stretched out. He was bandaged. Bandaged? What did that mean? Ty looked up at Dr. Doyle and back at Minus.

Thump ...Minus's tail gave a tiny wag.

He was alive!

His dog was alive! Minus!

Ty threw himself on the dog, touching the dog's head, sobbing and sobbing.

"Be careful," said Dr. Doyle. "He's very weak."

"We all thought he was going to die," said Eva, smiling through her own tears. "He lost so much blood. But Father came back just in time and operated and took the bullet out. Only a surgeon as skilled as Father could have done it." She looked at her father proudly.

Ty turned his tear-wet face to Dr. Doyle. "Oh sir," he said, his voice breaking. "Oh Doctor..."

Dr. Doyle knew what the boy was trying to say. The doctor looked away too because he was afraid of his own tears. He'd operated thousands of times, and saved many lives, oh but this success was particularly sweet.

"He needs rest," said Dr. Doyle gently. "Let's get breakfast."

Ty shook his head. "I'm not going to leave him," he said.

"I'll bring you some breakfast then," said Mrs. Doyle.

Ty lovingly stroked his dog. Tears kept coming down his face. Minus was alive. Just then Angel stalked into the room and over to the couch. In one second he had jumped up at the end of the couch, turned around once and curled up to sleep at the dog's feet. Ty smiled through his tears.

Eva walked up to Ty and put her hand on his shoulder. "Ty, I have some wonderful news," she said.

Ty looked up at her. She was smiling.

"Mother said that you can stay with us forever," said Eva.

"But my Pa..." said Ty.

"Mother will work it out."

Ty, overwhelmed, bent over Minus. Everything would work out, everything would be fine, his dog was alive.

***

The next day Mrs. Doyle took Ty and Mr. John Douville, a lawyer, up the hill to Ty's pa's house. Ty didn't want to go. First of all, he didn't want to leave Minus. He'd slept on the floor next to his dog all night. And Ty never wanted to see Pa and his brothers again. Mrs. Doyle, however, had insisted.

"We're going to do a very important thing to-day," she told him. "Mr. Douville is accompanying us to present legal papers. You must be strong."

Strong? Ty was terrified.

As they approached the house where he'd lived for the past few years, Ty thought it looked especially shabby and neglected. Had it always looked that way? Mrs. Doyle knocked on the door, and when no one answered, she pushed it open. Ty heard Mrs. Doyle give a little gasp when she saw the squalid conditions inside. Garbage was strewn around the floor, rotting food on the table. Empty bottles lay everywhere. Where was everyone?

Mr. Douville looked apprehensive. He had expected this to be a run-of-the-mill meeting. What sort of man could live in these conditions? And all those empty liquor bottles!

"Hello?" Mrs. Doyle called out. Just then Ty's pa came out of the back room. In his hand was a battered old suitcase and it appeared as if he had been stuffing clothes into it.

He looked startled when he saw Ty with Mrs. Doyle and the lawyer. Ty knew right away that he was not drunk. His pa got a certain look in his eye when he was drunk. Now he looked tired, worn, dirty, disheveled and like a beaten man. He hadn't shaved, and his hair was long and uncombed.

"What do you want?" Pa mumbled. "Me and Sam and Fred are leaving. Jake Fisher told me last night the Portland Logging Company will hire us if we can get down there by Friday."

"What do you propose to do with Ty?" asked Mrs. Doyle.

Pa shrugged. "There's an orphanage in Olympia."

"Why would you put your own son in an orphanage?" Mrs. Doyle asked.

Pa paused and, in a low voice, said, "His ma made me promise to take care of him, on her deathbed. He was so little and scrawny back then, and I couldn't get rid of my own flesh and blood, could I? But look at him. He's no kin of mine."

Pa looked at Ty then – stared at him, really – and Ty was taken aback at the anger he saw. "I can tell," he said to Ty. "Your ma didn't do right by me. She always thought she was too good for me. But it turned out she weren't so good after all."

Mrs. Doyle gave another little sharp intake of air. "Well. That is why we are here," she said. "I'd like you to sign these papers giving me custody of the boy. Sign here." Mr. Douville produced papers and a pen from his briefcase.

Pa gave a short hard laugh and looked at Mrs. Doyle. "I ain't signing anything. He can just go to the orphanage. He's bad luck just like his ma."

Ty's brain started working. This pathetic man before him, the one he used to think was his father, had made a mistake, a mistake that would give Ty his freedom.

"You just said that you're not related to me," said Ty, his voice trembling a little. "So, you have no rights."

Mrs. Doyle smiled a victorious smile. Ty was right. "Good job, Ty. Mr. Ritter, whereas a signature would be nice, it is not necessary," she said. "But let me tell you sir, that if you don't sign, I'm prepared to go to the police to report your abuse and neglect of this child. I have people who will give witness to your abhorrent treatment of him. You won't be going to Oregon, you won't be going anywhere except jail."

Ty didn't know exactly who these witnesses were, or if she was bluffing or if the police even cared, but it fooled his pa.

The man swore and grabbed the papers from the lawyer. He scrawled his signature and then threw the papers on the ground. With great dignity, Mrs. Doyle picked them up.

"Thank you," she said. "Ty, do you want to say anything to him?"

Ty looked at the man he had supposed was his father. He had so much to say, beginning with 'Would it have hurt you to be nice to a little boy?' But instead he stood there, looking at the pathetic man before him and just shook his head.

Mrs. Doyle took Ty by the hand and led him out the door. Mr. Douville followed.

As they made their way down the hill, Ty knew that the only pa he'd ever known would never bother him ever again. The man had lost all power. That thought should have delighted Ty, but to tell the truth, he was just so tired and sad, he didn't feel much of anything.

CHAPTER 25: HOP SUN ALWAYS SAID

The winds of the heavens shift suddenly;
so does human fate.

Ty spent that night in Li's old room with Minus sleeping on a soft blanket next to Ty's bed. Dr. Doyle had carefully carried Minus out of the restaurant office, back to their house. Ty stayed by his side all day. Now, at night, he watched his dog sleep and marveled that he was breathing regularly. Ty blinked and squinted to keep the tears back, his love was so overwhelming. He made himself think about numbers so he wouldn't start crying. He tried to figure out how many days he'd known Minus. He'd found the dog on April 17, there were thirty days in that month, so 13 left in that month...and...

Ty stroked his dog over and over and over. This was heaven. Life had changed so much in the last six months. Before, it was like he'd been encrusted in dirt and mud, living in darkness. When Minus and Eva came along – and Mrs. Doyle, Mr. and Mrs. Low, Hop Sun, and Li – that crust cracked open and he started living in sunshine. Ty put his face down into Minus's fur, and breathed in his good doggy smell. Then, with his hand resting on his dog's head, he slept.

Eva woke him the next morning when she came in carrying a tray with breakfast on it. She was grinning widely, her eyes happy.

"We are staying in this town for good," Eva told him. "Mother owns a building here, after all. But she's going to change it from a restaurant to an office building. Father will have his office in the front. Mother's office will be in the back. We just had to stay here. You know, New York has lots of doctors, but Tacoma has only one type-writer."

***

Months later, on a rainy March day, a letter came to the Doyles' house. The postmark was from Canada. It was from Mr. Low. It said:

Dear friends,

We wish to let you know what has become of us after our hasty exit from Tacoma. First of all, we all are well. We named our daughter Chang-chang which in Chinese means "flourishing." And she is flourishing greatly here in Canada. Never have we seen a more delightful child. She is truly blessed, as we are blessed as parents.

With the money Mrs. Doyle paid for my res-taurant, I was able to book passage on a ship

from Seattle to Victoria. By a wondrous coincidence, we met up with Hop Sun and Li who had been able to buy their tickets because of Ty's generosity. Together all of us journeyed to a little town where I knew some of the Chinese men in business. I was able to start another small restaurant, and Hop Sun agreed to be my cook. We are all thankful he is not the waiter.

Now that Mrs. Low is no longer confined to bed, she has taken charge of the baby, the restaurant, my life, and most of Canada. For such a small spark, she makes a great fire.

In closing, we ask that you not forget us. We look forward to the day when we can be reunited and when you will see again our Changchang. A Chinese proverb says "A child's life is like a piece a paper on which every person leaves a mark." You have already made a most wonderful mark on our daughter.

We think of you often.

Sincerely,

Mr. Low and family

P.S. Enclosed is a photograph of Mrs. Low and our beloved Changchang.

Li also wrote them a letter (dictated to Mr. Low) and enclosed a tea towel she had embroidered. On the tea towel was a three-legged dog that looked very much like Minus.

My dear friends,

My husband Hop Sun and I send you greetings. We live close to Mr. and Mrs. Low and their daughter. Hop Sun cooks at the restaurant, and I embroider tea towels and tablecloths to be sold at various shops. I was able to write my parents to inform them of what has happened to me and where I currently live. I am happy to send them money.

We hope that someday you will be able to visit us. Hop Sun said he will prepare a feast like none other when you come. We work hard, and we are happy.

We remain your faithful friends,
Li and Hop Sun
***

Ty immediately wrote a letter back to Hop Sun, Li and the Lows. He wrote it all by himself with just a little help from Eva.

Dear Friends,
I am good.
Minus is good.
Angel is good.

I have lots to eat.
I play chess with Dr. Doyle.
Hop Sun said everything will work out.
It did.
Your friend,
Ty

After he wrote that note, Ty lay in his bed in Li's old room and thought about all that had happened in less than a year. Really, he had a whole new life. Now, Minus, snoring lightly, lay on the braided rug next to him. Angel slept too, curled up at the end of the bed just out of easy reach. Ty could hear the spring rain splashing on the roof. Outside was rainy, raw, miserable. Inside, he was warm, dry, happy.

He scratched the top of his dog's head. Minus didn't open his eyes, he just sighed happily and resumed snoring. Ty remembered Mrs. Low making up her own proverb about Minus: "Sometimes that which is not perfect is perfect." Minus was about as perfect as a dog could be.

Ty took a deep breath of contentment and then stretched down to pet Angel three times. He stopped and kept his hand on the cat's back until he heard the best sound in the entire world: Angel's soft, vibrating purr.

What proverb would Ty make up about his life? He thought for a few seconds and then gave a little laugh. His proverb was more like a math problem than a wise saying. Still, Ty felt it summed up everything he'd learned this past year:

"Dog + Cat + Food + Family = Home."

THE END

Author's Note:

The Wind Will Not Stop is historical fiction. While I tried to be as accurate as I could about the facts, I invented most of the characters and a few events (inspired, of course, by real people and events).

Most specifically, near the book's end when the Mayor is hosting a great anti-Chinese rally (which DID take place), as far as I know nobody acted to disrupt the rally. This is just my wishful thinking...and something I know Eva would have loved to organize.

Also, I wanted to note that throughout the book I refer to Native Americans as "Indians." (When I could, I used a specific tribe "Puyallup Tribe of Indians.") The people living in 1885 would have referred to the indigenous people of Washington Territory as "Indians," and so, to be historically accurate, I used that term.

Some real events included in the book: At one point in the 1800s, several boys were sucked into a sand hill; a couple of them died. There was one woman who owned the only typewriter in town. Chinese men were smuggled by Jacob Ure from Canada to the United States, and indeed, he did tie them together so he could dump them into the water if the police approached him. The Chinese in Tacoma did have a banquet in which the white men who attended made fun of them. A bomb set by the anti-Chinese at a mill did explode. Saddest of all, Chinese women really were kidnapped from their homeland and brought to America to be prostitutes. If any tried to run away, the Tong tracked them down.

Tacoma was one of many towns in the West that forced their Chinese residents out. Sometimes people were killed. Lives were ruined. Businesses were destroyed.

Why should we care about this now? That's the question I was interested in and one that I hope you'll think about. Why is it important to learn about these historical events? It was a different time, wasn't it? Yet we still seem to struggle with people who are different than we are. As I write this, people of Asian descent are being targeted in acts of hate and violence. I had hoped those times were over.

As the Chinese proverb says, "We must learn from history."

One final question to think about: What would you have done, what would you have felt,

if you had lived in Tacoma during those turbu‐
lent months in 1885? Would you have had the
courage to help?

I've wondered that myself.

– Judy Carlson Hulbert

*by the Board of the Chinese Reconciliation
Project Foundation*

*The Wind Will Not Stop is a captivating story
about young people who witness an adult world
full of injustice. Though they cannot stop the historical events described in this tale – the expulsion of the entire Chinese population of a town
in 1885 – they resist it and they make a difference in the lives of their friends. Ty, the illiterate
young boy living with his violent father and
brothers, discovers a friend in Eva, the sophisti-
cated young girl who has moved with her mother
from New York City to Tacoma, a muddy nowhere at the end of the Northern Pacific Railroad on the shores of Puget Sound. Eva sees the
promise and talent inside Ty, who has not yet
learned to believe in himself. Eva and Ty meet a
number of memorable Chinese residents – a restaurant owner and his remarkable wife, an eter-
nally optimistic laborer and a young woman on*

the run from those who would enslave her. Together they determine to get involved and to try to stop the anti-Chinese movement that threatens the lives of their friends.

Author Judy Carlson Hulbert has carefully woven her story out of real events and real characters such as Mayor Jacob Weisbach, the instigator of what became known as "The Tacoma Method." The Chinese characters are fictional but are based upon the testimony of six merchants expelled from Tacoma at that time as well as historical maps showing where Chinese businesses were in 1885. The Chinese are vividly drawn both through their vibrant and varied characters as well as the author's careful attention to Cantonese culture including details of food, weddings, gender and class roles, and dozens of nicely translated proverbs.

Today, Tacoma is the only major city on the West Coast with no "Chinatown." Seattle, Portland, San Francisco, Los Angeles and Vancouver, B.C., have thriving Chinese communities whose origins go back to the Gold Rush days of the 1850s. Tacoma, too, had a burgeoning community of Chinese – mostly male laborers who had come to the United States on contracts to build the transcontinental railroads. In 1873, the Northern Pacific Railroad arrived in the Puget Sound area and its terminus was Tacoma – thus the slogan: "Tacoma, the City of Destiny." When it was completed, Chinese railroad workers became loggers, miners, farmers, lumber mill workers, store owners, labor contractors, restaurateurs, and laundry business owners. By 1885, about 1000 Chinese lived in Pierce County and 700 out of Tacoma's 7000 people were Chinese! But Tacoma's destiny turned out to be infamy, as the forced removal of the last group of Chinese on November 3, 1885 became an international scandal, embarrassing the United States government in its failure to protect Chinese citizens under its treaty obligations with the Chinese Qing Empire. A federal trial was held, in fact several in subsequent months, but each ended in a technicality. Not a single instigator went to jail over "The Tacoma Method" and they returned home as local heroes.

By this time, Seattle was the terminus of the Great Northern Railroad, the second rail line to Puget Sound, and Tacoma was left with a tarnished reputation that gave investors and prospective immigrants concern. Seattle grew to become the actual City of Destiny, not Tacoma.

Tacoma never again hosted a prosperous Chinatown. The Japanese community that gradually established a thriving community by the 1930s was decimated by the Japanese Internments during World War II and it too largely faded as its former members chose other cities. Later immigrant arrivals, often the result of military service on the local bases, included Koreans, Vietnamese, Cambodians, Laotians and many groups of Pacific Islanders.

When David and Signy Murdoch moved to Tacoma in 1982, they sensed something was amiss. After learning about the Chinese expulsion, Dr. Murdoch said, "Then it clicked because

... if a family member has been hurt, ostracized or embarrassed, that has an effect on the family for years." Dr. Murdoch joined with City councilman Robert Evans, former State Rep. Art Wang (D-Tacoma) and community activists in 1992 to initiate the reconciliation process. They formed a citizens committee which included Suzanne Barnett, Lorraine Hildebrand, Yuen Hi Ho, Theresa Pan Hosley, Bob Mack, Dr. George Tanbara, Jim Tsang, Sulja Warnick and Li-huang Wung, assisted by the city's planning and development services department staff Bart Alford and Martin Blackman and with support of Mayor Karen Vialle, the City Council and city manager Ray Corpuz. They spent 14 months planning, making community contacts and creating a preliminary design to commemorate the historic event in a park setting.

On November 30, 1993, the City Council unanimously approved Resolution No. 32415 to acknowledge that the 1885 expulsion was "a most reprehensible occurrence." The City Coun-

cil recognized the efforts of the citizens committee and endorsed the concept of building a Chinese commemorative park and international pavilion at the former National Guard site on Commencement Bay. Appropriately, the property is near the site of the early Chinese settlement called Little Canton. The City Council authorized the expenditure of $25,000 for preliminary site plans, preliminary cost estimate, and project programming for the project.

The Chinese Reconciliation Project Foundation (CRPF) was founded in Spring, 1994 to continue the reconciliation process. CRPF is a nonprofit organization that advances civic harmony by way of the Tacoma Chinese Reconciliation Park on Schuster Parkway along Commencement Bay. The Chinese garden motif allows the park to stand both as an acknowledgment of the forceful expulsion of the Chinese population of the City of Tacoma by municipal leaders and a large crowd on November 3, 1885, and as a celebration of the city's multicultural past, present, and future. The expulsion was an act of exclusion in response to complex conditions of the time, among them economic decline and anti-Chinese sentiment. The park is an act of reconciliation and inclusivity toward appreciation of the people of diverse legacies and interests who are part of the city as a dynamic community.

CRPF is proud to partner with author Judy Carlson Hulbert in publishing this remarkable and moving story to make sure that young readers today can discover this history and think about the issues that confronted the young protagonists in the book – how to resist and combat injustice in your own community. This publication is supported by a grant from Tacoma Creates, whose financial assistance is here gratefully acknowledged.

The modern City of Tacoma would please the young characters in <u>The Wind Will Not Stop</u>. They would find the rich variety of cultures and the stories of people from all over the world exciting. We can imagine Ty and Eva, *picnicking with her parents in Tacoma's Chinese Reconciliation Park, with Minus frolicking about, chasing seagulls and running through the Fuzhou Ting – the elegant Chinese pavilion that is the gift of the Tacoma's Chinese Sister City of Fuzhou. As they gaze at the ships from all over the world anchored in Commencement Bay, they would believe that Tacoma had grown closer to the goal of what they, in their youthful sense of justice, knew it could be – a city of destiny that is a home to a diverse and harmonious community of people.*

ACKNOWLEDGMENTS

I'd like to thank all the people who read and commented on any one of my many drafts:

* Andrea Klett Lynch, Karen York, Karen's insightful Mason Middle School book group, Phyllis Schneider, Lynn Raisl, Robin Strong, Lily Koblenz, Jill Sousa, Lara Henricksen, Mark Dahl, Leigh Kilgore, Pat Lautenschlager, Lissa Valentine, Joni Joachims, Carole Breitenbach (and Bill), Lotus Perry, Randy Perry, & Greg Youtz.

*My family Duane Hulbert, Annette Hulbert, Evan Hulbert & Neil Hulbert for their multiple readings and years of love. Special thanks to Neil Hulbert for technical help as well as math & chess info.

*My parents Ted and Swannie Carlson for all of their support throughout the years.

*Henry and August for giving me joyous breaks. (Jimmy too!)

*Linda Konner for publishing advice.

*Rebecca Young for proof-reading/copy-editing and graphic design work.

*Joni Joachims for creating the cover illustration and for our many discussions about art and creative endeavors. Also Chase Takata and Celia Hamburg for modeling.

*Finally, heartfelt thanks to my publisher: the Chinese Reconciliation Project Foundation (specifically Theresa Pan Hosley, Lotus Perry, and Greg Youtz) and Tacoma Creates.